Max Elliot Anderson

D1302233

Newspaper Caper

Tweener Press

Grand Haven, Michigan 49417

Newspaper Caper
By Max Elliot Anderson

Printed in the United States of America
Cover: Paul S. Trittin

Library of Congress Control Number: 2003110541
ISBN: 0-9729256-4-3

Baker Trittin Concepts
Tweener Press Division
P.O. Box 20
Grand Haven, Michigan 49417

(616) 846-8550

http://www.gospelstoryteller.com
btconcepts@ameritech.net

To my parents

Ken and Doris Anderson

who have written so many important chapters

in my life.

Chapter 1

Anyone who knew Tom Stevens was sure of one thing. The boy was going places. In the twelve years he had lived so far, Tom already showed signs of becoming a master salesman.

"I believe you could sell anything to anyone anytime you wanted to," his father often told him.

The Stevens family lived in Rock Island, Illinois, not far from the Mississippi River.

Tom organized his two best friends, Jimmy Wilson and Matt Woodridge, into an aluminum can recycling powerhouse back when they were just nine years old. When he was only four, Tom was the first boy on his street to set up a lemonade stand ... in January. And even though snow already covered the ground, people still stopped and bought some. He could just as easily sell hot chocolate on the most sweltering day of the summer if he wanted to.

When he decided to go door-to-door selling magazine subscriptions at the age of ten, his parents were embarrassed at how much money their neighbors handed over to Tom. He even managed to sell copies of old newspapers to his own father when Tom was just five years old. His dad thought it was all in fun, but to Tom, this was serious business.

So it came as no surprise when he decided to start delivering newspapers. Not just a starter route either. Tom took over three established routes. At first his friends took turns helping Monday through Saturday, but since the Sunday paper was usually three times the normal size and weight, with all those circulars, special sections, and of course, the comics, Tom, Jimmy and Matt did those together. He paid them too. Now they all worked together every morning.

All three boys planned to go out for football next fall. Tom wanted to try out for quarterback. Jimmy had strong legs and broad shoulders. He was perfect for halfback. Matt, with his short, stocky build, and those extra pounds, planned to play center. They even dreamed of going all the way through college playing football together. That's the kind of friends they were.

"Learn the value of a dollar," Tom's father always told him.

That was easy for him to say, Tom thought. His dad was still in bed by the time over half of their papers were already delivered.

"This route will help us with exercise, strength training, and breathing," Tom told his friends. "We'll be in the best shape of anyone else on the whole team this year."

But that would have to wait until fall. Right now they were beginning to enjoy their summer vacation. Well, "enjoy" might be too strong a word.

"We have to get out of bed at four in the morning to put these papers together and roll them up before we ever hit the streets," Matt complained while sitting in front of a giant stack of Sunday papers he could hardly see over.

"But just think of all the other centers who are sleeping in this morning," Tom told him. That was all his friend needed to hear, and he worked twice as hard.

"After we get to high school, maybe we can buy a car and deliver even more papers," Tom added.

"Hey, between the football scholarships we'll all get, and the money we make from now till then delivering papers, we're gonna be rich!" Jimmy hollered.

"Keep it down," Tom cautioned. "What are you trying to do? Wake up the whole neighborhood? Besides, my Dad told me I could only take these routes if it didn't interfere with his beauty sleep. Or was that my mom? I forget."

"Let's get a move on," Matt encouraged. "We have to finish in time for Sunday school."

Soon the boys rode off together, their bikes loaded down like pack mules carrying cloth bags brimming with papers. Tom had it all figured. Since Matt was such a big guy, they stuffed his bike with as many bags as it could hold. Then he had four more strapped around his neck and shoulders. Jimmy and Tom also carried bags, but not nearly as many. They rode side-by-side down each street. One tossed papers to all the odd-numbered houses while the other hit the even-numbered. "Hit" doesn't totally cover it. Occasionally, a flowerpot took a direct hit, but so far no windows had been broken. Each time they went out, the two boys tossed their papers with greater accuracy.

Matt plodded slowly behind them, ready to re-supply whenever he was needed. Tom thought that throwing papers was good practice for the future game-winning touchdown passes he planned to make.

"Watch this," he announced. Then he rifled his paper onto the front porch of a two-story house with a well-manicured lawn. It landed right in the middle of the welcome mat. "Hey Matt," Tom called out. "I didn't know you had so many friends in this neighborhood."

"I do?"

"Sure."

"I don't know any of these people. Honest."

"Oh, I don't know about that. There's a welcome *mat*, and there's another welcome *mat*, and another and another."

Matt just smiled back. He was too busy peddling his heavy load.

The entire route took the boys three full hours. There were the usual hazards to watch out for. Each boy carried a can of pepper spray for any dog dumb enough to come near, and a loud air horn in case the spray missed its mark. But Matt had already lost three pairs of his best jeans to a vicious dog that lived over on Maple Street. That's because Matt was the slowest, and because it was impossible, with all the extra papers he carried, for him to let go of his handlebars long enough to defend himself. The other boys had to act like fighter jets guarding a bomber plane, but sometimes, they were just a few seconds too late and Matt was out another pair of pants.

The boys neared Maple when they heard that familiar sound. It was getting louder and, for sure, it was coming closer. Jimmy and Tom didn't know it, but this time, Matt had a secret weapon for the dog. As that ugly, slobbering mongrel was about to take a chomp out of his right leg, Matt quickly pulled a paper bag from inside his jacket. He almost lost his balance but was able to grab the handlebar again just in time to keep from falling. Matt's friends watched as he flipped his bag toward the dog. Immediately the hound stopped chasing the boys.

He had a look in his eyes that said, "Hummm, wonder what's in the sack?"

As the boys rode away they watched him rip the flimsy paper bag apart to reveal a large hunk of fresh meat.

9

"That better not be your mom's Sunday dinner," Tom warned.

"Nope. She bought it for me special." Once they were at a safe distance, Matt eased his bike to a stop and the others joined him. They continued watching as the dog that had plagued them on so many mornings grabbed the roast with his sharp teeth, tossed it in the air, caught it, then practically swallowed the thing whole.

"Now comes the fun part," Matt chuckled.

At first the dog just stood there. Then he sat down in the middle of the street. Then he got up. Then he sat down again. All of a sudden he let out a whoop louder than any ambulance or fire truck the boys had ever heard in all the days they'd been delivering papers. That poor dog took off like he was running the hundred-yard dash. The boys could still hear the pooch howling even though he was already blocks away.

"What's wrong with him, Matt?" Tom asked.

"Nothing that about a thousand gallons of water won't cure."

"Did you put something on the meat?" Jimmy asked.

Matt grinned slyly. "Oh, I think I did."

"What was it?"

"First, I soaked it overnight in the juice from a jar of jalapeno peppers. Then I took a bottle of Tabasco sauce, and finished it off with white pepper."

"Man, that's going to be one sick puppy."

"You're right, Tom" Matt agreed. "But not because it's so hot."

"Why then?" Jimmy asked.

"Matt. You didn't!" Tom demanded.

"'Fraid I did."

"What?" Jimmy prodded.

"I took a bunch of laxatives and crammed them into some holes I made in it."

"Matt!" Jimmy scolded.

"All I can tell you is his owners are going to be really upset when he comes home, lays down on the kitchen floor, and..."

For the next three full blocks the boys couldn't stop laughing as they continued delivering their papers.

Chapter 2

Their delivery routes took them past some interesting places. Customers included a firehouse, a police station, a few businesses, and endless rows of houses. But their favorite stop had to be Big Bob's Doughnut Shop. There they were treated to a free doughnut and orange juice every morning. Matt usually got to have two. Along the route the boys often saw some pretty strange things, but they adopted a sort of newspaper carrier's code of silence. Still it was hard not to be able to tell anyone when they'd seen customers locked outside their front doors. These people weren't always exactly dressed to meet the day either. One time Matt saw a woman with curlers in her hair and some kind of green goo all over her face. It made him scream, and when he did, she did too. He almost fell off his bike when that happened, and the woman wound up in her rose bushes.

But most of the time they minded their own business

and stuck to the job of their deliveries. After all, that's what they got paid for.

Then early one morning, everything was going just fine when they saw something that didn't look right. It was still dark as the boys turned down Kishwaukee Street. A man had just finished backing a tow truck up to an expensive looking car. When the man climbed out of his truck, Tom thought he acted nervous. From the light inside the cab, Tom also noticed another man sitting there. He wore a light blue shirt with a nametag on the front and a patch on the sleeve. The man had dark hair. He kept his face hidden but Tom saw the name on his shirt "Jake."

The man outside the truck could have used a shave, his shirt and pants were greasy, and he had an unlit cigar clamped between his teeth. But when he saw the boys he did something strange. Instead of hooking the car up to the back of his truck, he quickly looked around, then jumped back in the cab and drove away. His tires squealed on the pavement leaving a cloud of blue smoke in the early morning air.

"That's odd," Jimmy commented. "Did you guys get the name on his truck?"

"I did," Tom answered. "It said 'Smitty's Towing.'"

"Why'd he take off like that?" Matt asked.

Tom thought about it for a moment. "I wonder if it has anything to do with an article I saw in the paper today."

"What article?" Matt asked.

"You guys know how I like to read stuff while we roll our papers in the morning?"

"Yeah," Jimmy laughed. "The first couple times we were late because of it. You're supposed to *deliver* the paper, not read it clear through."

"I know. But there was something about this story."

"Wouldya tell us or what?" Matt demanded.

"Pull up to that corner. I'll show you."

The boys steered their bikes to the curb, eased them down on the ground, and sat together on a bench. Tom slipped a paper from one of the cloth bags. "I can't remember what section it was in." He quickly scanned each page then flipped to the next. "Not here," he reported. Then he turned to the local section. "There it is."

"There what is?" Jimmy asked.

"Couldya read it?" Matt begged.

Tom began, "Cars mysteriously missing. Police report a rash of unexplained car thefts in our city."

"People probably just forgot where they parked them," Jimmy suggested.

Tom continued. "Authorities are reminding residents to lock their cars, install alarms and anti-theft devices. Cars disappear primarily in the overnight hours. Park in well-lighted areas. Residents are encouraged to report any suspicious activity in their neighborhoods."

Even though it was a warm morning, that last statement sent a chill right up Tom's back. *I wonder*, he thought.

"So whadaya think?" Matt asked.

"I think we'd better get back on our bikes if we expect to finish on time." But as they rode away, Tom could think of nothing except the article. That, and the scary looking guy sitting in the wrecker. *I hope I never see that face again,* he thought.

It was pretty obvious his mind was no longer on his work because twice he turned and began riding his bike down an alley. Tom reached in his bag and threw papers into an empty lot, an abandoned car, and a dumpster before his friends were able to stop him.

"What's wrong with you?" Jimmy asked.

"Huh?"

"Now we have to go back and get those papers you tossed, and I *am not* climbing into any dumpster. That'll have to be your job."

"I'm sorry. I just can't..." But Tom didn't finish his sentence.

For the rest of the morning, not another word was spoken. Finally, the boys returned to Tom's house and coasted into the driveway.

"You guys wanna come over after church? We could mess around or something."

"We gotta visit my grandma today," Jimmy complained.

"And I have to go feed the ants," Matt added.

"What are you talking about?" Jimmy asked.

"Feed the ants. You know. A picnic."

"All right. I'll see you tomorrow morning."

"Don't remind us," they groaned together.

After his friends sped away, Tom took a leftover copy of the paper and thumbed through the pages until he came to that article again. He began reading, "Inspector Vanderwaal is seeking assistance from the public in fighting motor vehicle thefts in the area." The inspector continued, "The number of stolen cars has steadily increased in all sectors and car owners must be more vigilant in both protecting their property and reporting any thefts immediately."

"Wow," Tom whispered. As he continued reading the article, a loud sound startled him. He jumped up so fast he threw his newspaper high into the air.

While the pages floated gently back to the ground, his father asked, "Why so jumpy?"

"Nothin'. You scared me, that's all."

"What were you reading?"

"Just a story."

"Well, we have to head for church. Are you ready?"

"Sure."

"Then hurry and pick up your papers. Mom will be out in a minute."

Tom found the page again with the article he'd been reading. He quickly tore it out, folded it, and slipped it in his pocket. After church the family ate dinner together, but Tom didn't gobble his food like usual. He spent more time pushing things around on his plate.

"Don't you like it, Tom?" his mother asked.

"Like what?"

"The food I fixed for you?"

"No."

She looked surprised.

"I mean it isn't the food ... I'm sorry." He proceeded to pick up speed until he finished his dinner at about the same time as his parents finished theirs.

"Who's ready for cherry pie?" his mother asked.

"Could I be excused?"

Tom's father took a long look at him. "Really? But you love cherry pie."

"Would it be okay if I went out for a couple hours? I'd like to check on something."

"Is it important?" his father asked.

"Kinda."

"Then just make sure you're home before dark."

"Oh, I will. Don't worry."

"You have to get up early," his mother reminded.

"Don't I know it. Thanks."

Tom scampered out through the kitchen. He stopped for a moment to stare at the fresh, hot, cherry pie cooling on the counter. *Can't believe I'm passing that up*, he thought. Then he pushed open the screen door and headed for his beat up bike.

As he coasted down the street, Tom continued to replay the newspaper article over and over in his head. He felt like there was something big going on right in his own town. Even though he wasn't a reporter, Tom thought there might be something he could do. So he peddled toward the fire station.

He knew all the firemen there and they knew him. But Tom hoped his special friend would be on duty today. He usually was on Sunday afternoons. Tom rolled up to the enormous red doors that were always open on warm days, just waiting for the next call. Inside he saw all the gleaming fire equipment. The trucks in his town were painted bright yellow with chrome so polished he could see his freckled face in it.

He stopped to pat Smokey, the Dalmatian, on his head. Smokey especially liked it when Tom scratched his ears. It made the lovable dog grunt just like a pig in the mud. Usually Tom spent a long time playing with Smokey, but today he had other things on his mind. He turned to see if his friend was sitting in his usual place. And he was.

19

Tom stood up and walked over to a chair that was propped up against a light green wall where several firemen's black uniforms hung on large hooks.

Tom cleared his throat so he wouldn't frighten his friend, but the man didn't move. So Tom reached out and slowly pushed open one eyelid of the little man with white hair and a thin, white mustache.

"Buster?" Tom asked. "You in there?"

The man snorted. He smacked his lips and then snorted again. As Tom watched, his friend managed to open the other eye by himself.

"And who wants to know?" Buster asked as he pushed his hat toward the back of his head.

"You know who it is."

"Let me think. Is it the President of the United States?"

"No, it is not," Tom responded defiantly.

"The mayor then."

"Wrong again."

"The chief?"

"Only one guess left."

"Let's see. Wouldn't want to waste one. It's my good friend, Tommy."

"Right."

"So what brings you down here on such a nice lazy day?" Buster asked.

"I have a question."

"Don't you always?"

"I know, but this one's kind of important."

"You mean all the others have been just for fun?"

"Well, no. It's just that this time..." Tom struggled, "You're confusing me."

"Okay then. What would you like to know?" Buster asked. "I got the whole day."

"It's hard to know where to start."

Buster shrugged his shoulders. "Just try."

"Well, what do you know about stealing cars?"

Buster nearly fell out of his chair. He had to grab hold of one of the uniforms hanging next to where he was sitting or he would have sprawled right out on the floor.

"You're asking me how to steal a car? What makes you think I know how, and even if I did, why in the world would I tell you?"

Tom reached into his back pocket and pulled out the folded piece of paper. "Here. Read this."

Buster held the article while he took a pair of wire-rimmed glasses out of his shirt pocket. Then he read about the stolen cars. When he finished he asked, "This still doesn't explain why you want to know how to do it?"

"I know. But suppose a person thought he saw something? Then what?"

"Guys see things all the time. It don't mean nothin'."

21

"I know, but..."

"If you make a mistake you might get somebody in a lot of trouble, even if they didn't do nothin' wrong."

"So what are you saying?"

"I'm saying be sure first. Be very sure."

"I will."

"Say," Buster added. "Don't you deliver to the police substation over on 6th?"

"Uh huh."

"I know the desk sergeant there, and he was telling me they have a new booklet that tells people how to keep their cars from getting stolen. You should stop by and pick up a copy."

Tom turned to leave. "Think I will."

"Tell him Buster sent you."

Tom decided to ride his bike over to where he'd seen the tow truck. When he came to the house, he noticed the car was gone.

"I knew it," he said.

He jumped off his bike and pushed it up the sidewalk to the front steps of the house. His heart started pounding but somehow, Tom had to know. His feet felt like two, heavy Sunday papers as he walked up the steps. When he reached out to ring the bell, the front door swung open.

"Time to collect again?" a nice woman asked. She wore an apron that had flour smeared on it. She held a rolling pin in one hand and a cloth in the other.

"N...no," Tom stammered. "I... I wanted to, to ask you a question."

"I thought you were my husband."

That made Tom's face turn red. "Do you usually greet him at the door with a rolling pin?"

She looked at it and smiled. "I'm just making a pie, but he should have been back by now."

"Back from where?"

"The police station."

"So it *was* stolen."

"What was stolen?" she asked.

"Your car."

"WHAT?"

"Your car. It was stolen. Wasn't it?"

"Oh this is terrible, simply terrible. How do you know it was stolen?"

"I saw it."

"When? Where?"

"Early in the morning. Right in front of your house."

"In front of this house? When?"

"This morning."

Just then Tom heard a car stop in the street behind him. He turned to see the same car the tow truck driver had stopped in front of.

"Wait a minute," Tom said. "Is that your car?"

"Yes."

"It isn't stolen."

"Well of course it isn't, you silly boy."

A man stepped out of the car, closed the door, and came up the walk. By now, Tom was embarrassed.

"Honey, this is our paper boy."

The man reached into the pocket of his jeans. "How much do we owe you today?"

"No sir. I'm not collecting."

The woman told her husband, "He said our car had been stolen."

"That's ridiculous. There it sits right where I parked it."

"I know. I must have made a mistake." Tom excused himself and ran to his bike. He might have made a mistake this time, but he knew something wasn't right.

On the way home he stopped at the police station to pick up a copy of the book Buster told him about. There was a whole box of them on the counter with a sign that read, "Take one." He started flipping through the pages and found that cars get stolen all the time. While he stood there reading, another officer walked into the station.

"Well, Jenkins," the officer said to the desk sergeant. "Another one's missing."

"Are you sure?" the sergeant asked.

"Positive."

Now Tom couldn't wait until morning so he could read the next article and see what was happening. He hurried home to call Jimmy and Matt.

Chapter 3

Tom ran out of the police station in such a hurry he didn't even bother to get on his bike at first. Instead, he yanked it out of the rack and began running down the street beside the bike.

This is dumb, he thought.

It was just that his mind was on the stolen cars and the fresh news he'd just heard. Tom almost felt like a real newspaper reporter at that moment, not someone who only delivered the news.

Once he hopped on his bike he rode as fast as his legs could peddle. When he got home he raced into the driveway and jumped off his bike while it was still moving, like a cowboy in a western movie who hops off his galloping horse. The bike continued rolling across the backyard all by itself until it ran right into the hedge.

Good thing we don't live on a lake, he thought. *I'd be sunk.*

He hurried through the back door and dashed up the stairs to his room. Right away he tried to call his friends, but then he remembered what they'd told him. Jimmy was with his grandmother, and Matt was out feeding the ants someplace. So Tom began reading the booklet he'd picked up. The more he read the more excited he became.

Finally, at around six in the evening, he decided to try his friends again. Jimmy answered on the second ring.

"Hello."

"Hey Jim, it's Tom."

"What's up?"

"I went to the police station today and got this book I think you're gonna want to see."

"What's it about?"

"About twenty-five pages."

"No, be serious."

"Just give Matt a call and come on over. I'll explain it when you guys get here."

"Okay. If he's home, we'll be over in a few minutes."

"See you then," Tom concluded, and hung up the phone. He decided to take his book and wait for them on the back steps. When the boys rode up they wanted to know what was so important that it couldn't wait until morning.

"I got sun burned today," Matt complained. "So this better be good."

"It is," Tom assured him. "I went to see Buster today,

and he told me about this new book I could get about stolen cars."

"What's it say?" Jimmy asked.

"Mostly it tells people how to keep their cars from driving off without them."

"So?" Matt muttered.

"So, did you know that a car gets stolen in America every twenty seconds?"

Jimmy held up his hand, "Wait a minute," he told them as he looked at his watch. "There goes another one," he announced after twenty seconds had passed.

"That means three every minute!" Matt exclaimed.

"I know," Tom added. "And we almost saw one of them get ripped off right in front of us."

"Whadaya think *we* can do about it?" Matt asked.

Tom shrugged his shoulders. "Hey, Jimmy. Doesn't your uncle own a garage or something?"

"Sure he does. So what?"

"Well, we could go see him after our deliveries in the morning."

"What for?" Jimmy asked.

"We can ask him about all the stolen cars and see if he knows anything about them."

"Wait a minute," Jimmy protested. "Are you trying to say my uncle is mixed up in this somehow? Because if you are, you're gonna be sorry."

"No, of course not. I just thought he might be able to tell us more about it. That's all."

"Come on you guys," Matt complained. "We gotta get up early tomorrow. I say we go home, go to bed, and talk about this in the morning."

"Fine with me," Tom agreed. "See you at four-thirty."

"Did you have to remind us?" Jimmy whined.

The two boys headed back home on their bikes, but Tom wasn't finished with his book. He continued reading about the things people could buy to stop the car thieves. Some of the alarm systems cost a lot of money. Later, after he'd climbed into bed, his mind refused to shut off. He kept thinking about Smitty's Towing and the scary man who drove the truck. Then he began counting off twenty seconds at a time. He couldn't believe how many cars that would be.

While I'm sleeping tonight, he thought, *that must be something like ... let me see.* Tom was good at math and he figured in his head that, at three cars per minute, it meant one hundred and eighty were stolen every hour across the country.

By the time I get up in eight hours, that means almost one thousand five hundred people will wake up and their cars won't be in the driveway.

That thought made Tom shudder. He pulled his blankets up tighter under his chin. Just then a loud truck drove past his house. The headlights drifted across the walls in his bedroom. He jumped out of bed and hurried to the window, expecting to see that spooky tow truck, but he was too late to see anything.

Now his room was completely dark again. Tom started thinking about what might be lurking under his bed, just waiting to grab him by his ankles if he came any closer. That thought sent goose bumps exploding all over his body.

I can't believe this, Tom thought. *I'm twelve years old, and us big kids aren't supposed to be afraid of something under the bed.* Unfortunately that didn't help. He still stood frozen in position. Then a car came down the street from the opposite direction. Its lights gave off enough of a glow that Tom could clearly see the edge of his bed, just for an instant. That was all the time he needed as he vaulted across the room and dove under his covers.

With a slightly nervous chuckle he thought, *There. I made it.* Not long after that he was asleep. Tom's alarm went off at four o'clock. It jolted him at first. He didn't feel very well rested. He also noticed his covers were mostly on the floor. *Must have been SOME dream,* he thought.

He quickly dressed and went quietly to the kitchen for a hurried breakfast. When he walked out the back door, his friends came riding up.

"I'm glad you guys don't trade off on the week days anymore."

"Not a chance," Matt said. "After all that talk about

stolen cars, we wouldn't want to miss anything."

"We're gonna do papers with you every day from now on," Jimmy added.

Tom began walking toward the front of his house. "Sounds good to me," he called back.

Each morning, while Tom slept, a newspaper truck drove around the city. It stopped along the way so a man in the back could toss bundles of papers in places where newspaper carriers, like Tom, picked them up. Tom found his papers in the driveway every morning.

"How do those guys know how many to give us?" Matt asked.

"Sometimes they drop off too many and sometimes not enough," Tom answered. He pulled a computer printout from his back pocket. "People are supposed to let the paper know when they go away on vacation and when they get back."

"Man," Jimmy sighed, "I'll bet burglars would love to get their hands on that list."

"They also know who's late in paying their bill, and the new people who move into a neighborhood and start taking the paper. But they can still mess it up."

"I think it's something how they keep track of all that," Matt commented.

The boys began hauling their heavy papers around to the garage. Tom cut the strings holding each bundle and dumped a stack in front of each of his friends. Then he took one for himself. Like working in a factory assembly line, Jimmy and Matt began quickly rolling up the papers and placing a rubber band around each one.

"Man I hate when it rains and we have to stick these dumb things in plastic bags. That takes like forever, huh Tom?" Jimmy complained.

But Tom didn't say anything. The boys looked up to see that their friend hadn't rolled any of his papers yet. He had only gotten as far as the first one on his pile. Tom was reading something again.

"Howdaya expect us to get all these papers ready if you're not helping?" Matt asked. Still Tom didn't answer. So Jimmy took one of his rolled up papers, tossed it across the garage, and hit the page Tom was reading. He looked up. "Hey, what's the big idea?"

"You aren't working," Matt complained.

Tom was a little flustered. "Oh, sorry. It's just that I was reading this story."

"What story?" Jimmy asked.

"Well, you remember the book I went to get yesterday?"

"From the police station," Matt added.

"Yeah. Well, while I was there a policeman came in and said the strangest thing."

"What?" Matt asked.

"He said, 'Well, Jenkins, another one's missing.'"

"Who's Jenkins?" Jimmy asked.

"That's not the important part. The policeman reached up and took a clipboard from a hook on the wall. They had a bunch of them, but the one he grabbed read 'Stolen Cars' on the cover."

"So? I still don't get it," Matt grumbled.

"This article gives the addresses of cars that are missing."

"That's it?"

"No. That's not it. When he put it back on the wall I read some of the names real quick. A bunch of them were taken from places right on our route."

"Cut it out," Matt complained. "You're starting to scare me."

"Well, all I'm saying is we need to keep our eyes open."

"Hey, no problem," Jimmy snickered. "You shut your eyes on a bike and you could smack into just about anything."

"I'm serious, guys. We might even get to solve this mystery."

Matt shuddered. "I think I'll just stick to delivering papers."

"Jimmy," Tom suggested. "Let's go see your uncle after we finish this morning."

Chapter 4

Tom and his friends rolled out of the driveway on their bikes and headed toward the first customers on their route. As usual, the streets were dark. Except for an occasional delivery truck, the boys were all alone. They chattered along the way and Tom felt like the time went quickly. Then suddenly, as their bikes turned down Maple Street, they heard that sound.

"You guys got your spray ready?" Tom asked.

"We won't need it," Matt answered.

"How do you figure?" Jimmy asked.

"I just have a feeling, that's all," Matt responded.

They listened while the bellowing from the scariest dog any of them had ever known kept coming closer.

Jimmy nervously cleared his throat. "Hey Matt, what are you gonna do if that mutt remembers you, and doesn't like what he remembers?"

"Oh, he'll remember. You can count on that. But I

think you'll be surprised."

They stopped their bikes to see what was going to happen next. Just then the slobbering beast burst out from between two houses. He ran straight toward Matt as if he planned to eat another pant leg sandwich. But then he did the strangest thing. Instead of bolting into the street, the dog took one look at Matt and suddenly dug the sharp claws on all four paws deep into the grass. He grabbed the dirt so hard it made him stop like a minivan in a crash test. But he'd been running so fast his body kept right on moving at full speed, which meant he fell to the ground and rolled all the way into the middle of the street.

"Matt! Look out," Tom warned as he reached for his spray can. But when the dog finally stopped rolling he flopped onto his back and looked straight up at Matt. Then he whimpered, rolled over, and got back on his feet.

"Run for it," Jimmy shouted. But Matt stayed still. The dog looked over to the other boys, looked back up at Matt, then he ran away as fast as he could go, howling like a little puppy.

"That's the most amazing thing I ever saw," Tom gasped. "How did you know what he'd do?"

My uncle in California trains animals to be in TV shows and movies. When I was having so much trouble with the Maple Street Mongrel, my mom called out there for some ideas. My uncle said that dogs are real smart. They can learn things from rewards and from punishment. I knew rewards wouldn't work, so I had to do something else to make him remember me."

"Well, it sure worked," Jimmy said. "Think you should tell the guys down at the post office?"

Matt agreed with a wide grin.

"We'd better get moving if we want to stop by my uncle's shop," Jimmy reminded. The boys turned their bikes around and headed off toward the next street.

After they delivered the last paper, Tom asked, "Is your uncle's place far from here?"

"Just a few blocks." Minutes later they coasted their bikes through the opened overhead door at P. J.'s Auto Repair. Jimmy's uncle stood behind the counter working on some papers. Everyone who worked in the shop wore a uniform. Dark blue pants, a light blue shirt with a patch on the sleeve, and name tags made it easy to know who worked there and who didn't.

"Morning, Uncle P. J."

"Hi, Jimmy. What brings you down here? Did you crash your bike or something?"

"No. But we could use some help."

"We?"

"My friends and I. Uncle P. J., this is Tom, and that's Matt."

"Nice to meet you boys. Now, what can I do for you?"

Tom moved closer to the counter. "We were wondering what you might know about stolen cars?"

"Stolen cars? Now why would you guys want to know about stealing cars?" he asked.

Just then Tom noticed one of the other mechanics watching them. He acted like he wasn't paying any attention, but Tom was sure he was listening to their conversation.

"Could we go someplace else and talk?" he asked.

"I'm sorry, but I have to work the counter this morning, and I'm expecting some deliveries from the auto parts store."

"Well," Tom continued. "We wondered what happens to cars after people steal them."

"The answer to that question is as different as the people involved. I know of some groups that steal to order."

"Steal to order?" Jimmy asked.

"A guy tells them what kind of car he wants, and they go out and get it for him. Shoot, they can even find the exact color he asks for."

Matt whistled.

"But unless it's just a bunch of kids out for a joyride, a lot of stolen cars wind up in a chop shop."

"What's that?" Tom asked.

A small van pulled up in front of the shop. A man, wearing a green uniform hopped out, opened the sliding door on the side, and pulled out several boxes. He brought the load into the shop and placed them on the counter.

"I don't know why you guys don't use armored cars," Uncle P. J. joked.

"What for?" the man asked.

"You'd think I was buying gold bars for what these parts cost."

"Don't look at me," the man protested. "I just deliver the stuff."

Jimmy's uncle signed a form the man had on a clipboard, and he was gone.

"Now where was I?" Uncle P. J. asked.

"You were talking about chop shops."

"Right." He picked up one of the boxes. "Now you take this replacement part here. It costs a hundred and eighty-nine bucks."

"Why so much?" Jimmy asked.

"Because only so many places make them. If you try to buy a cheaper one, it won't last. Then the customer gets mad and probably won't ever come back."

"But what does that have to do with a chop shop?" Tom asked.

"Let me see if I can explain it this way. When your parents go to buy a new car, it has a price on the window."

"Yeah, my dad says he thinks it's robbery," Matt chuckled.

"Well, did you know a car like that is worth more in

pieces than as a whole car?"

"How could that be?" Matt asked.

"Because replacement parts always cost more than the originals at the factory. Now, if I wasn't honest, I might get a few guys together and start stealing cars around town."

"What would you do with them?" Tom asked.

"I'd probably have them taken to a place that's hidden away. Inside we would take out all the parts, remove the doors, tires, seats, everything. We'd dump the shell on a street someplace, and we'd have all these free parts."

"That's amazing," Jimmy said.

"Well," his uncle continued, "I've heard that some of these guys make a deal with the owner of the car so when the shell *is* found, their insurance company pays up. Then everybody makes money."

"Except the insurance company," Tom suggested.

"Exactly."

Again Tom looked over to the worker who had now moved in a little closer. He was standing behind a shelf, pretending to arrange some of the boxes. Tom tried to remember where he had seen that man before.

"Have you been reading the stories in the paper?" Tom asked.

"I don't take the paper."

"You don't?" Jimmy exclaimed.

"Oh. Shouldn't have said that in front of three

carriers now should I?"

"We could sign you up right now," Matt offered.

Tom ran toward the door and called out, "I gotta get something." When he came back, he had one of the leftover newspapers. He opened it and pointed to an article. "Here, read this."

Uncle P. J. read for the next couple minutes. When he glanced up he had a worried look on his face. He turned to a bulletin board behind him and pulled off a sheet of paper.

"A police officer came around with these notices, only I didn't think much of it at the time. But now, with all the cars that have been stolen..."

"What do you think Uncle P. J.?" Jimmy asked.

"I think I'll start taking the paper for one thing."

"Yeah, but what about all those missing cars?"

"A chop shop?" Matt asked.

Just then the shadowy man behind the shelf knocked something to the floor. Everyone looked up to see what had happened as the man quickly leaned down to pick it up. But when he did that, Tom clearly read the name on his tag.

"Jake," he whispered. "I gotta go do something," Tom yelled as he ran back for his bike. "I'll call you guys later."

Tom hopped on his bike and headed for the library. He parked in the rack out front and hurried inside. He'd already been to the library several times for school projects. When he was younger, his mother used to bring him there for special programs.

Behind the information desk sat a woman who had black hair with gray streaks. She wore glasses and worked at a computer.

Tom walked up and cleared his throat.

"Yes. May I help you?"

"I'm looking for a book."

"Well then, you've come to the right place," she said cheerfully. "What kind of a book were you looking for?"

"I'm not exactly sure."

"What subject would it be?"

"I want to look up companies."

"The phone book would be good place to start."

"Yes, but I want more information than that."

"Is this a local company?"

"I think so."

"Then you need to go up on the second floor. At the help desk, ask for the City Registry."

"What's that?"

"It lists every business registered in town."

"That's what I want. Thank you." Tom rushed up the stairs, found the desk, and asked for the book. Since it was in the reference section, he had to read it at a table right there. First he opened the book to the different kinds of businesses. Then he went to the alphabetical listing. After searching for several minutes, Tom slowly closed the book.

"I knew it," he whispered.

Chapter 5

As soon as Tom returned home from the library he called his friends. Matt and Jimmy knew that any time their friend called there was no sense trying to say no to him. A few minutes later they were sitting together in Tom's room.

"Okay, Tom," Jimmy sighed. "What is it this time?"

"It better be important because I was just about to have a bowl of ice cream," Matt complained.

"And why did you run off like that from my uncle's shop?" Jimmy asked. "He's gonna wonder what kind of friends I have."

"Hey, wait a minute," Matt said. "I stayed with you."

Tom held up his hands for quiet. "Look. I can't tell you everything right now, but I think I know who's involved in stealing the cars."

Jimmy stood to his feet. "Now hold on a second. If you're about to blame my uncle again I'll..."

"No. It isn't him. Listen. I went to the library after I

left you guys."

Matt rolled his eyes. "How exciting."

"You might change your mind after you hear what I found out."

"So?" Jimmy challenged.

"I went to the place where they keep all the important information. They have a book that lists every company in town."

"Well what did you find?" Matt asked.

"It's what I didn't find."

"Are you trying to trick us?" Jimmy demanded.

"You remember the morning when we saw that tow truck?"

"Sure," Matt recalled. "The guy took off as soon as he saw us."

"Do you also remember the name on the door?"

"Smith's or something," Jimmy offered.

"Smitty's. The name was Smitty's. And guess what I found out?"

"I thought you said you didn't find anything."

"Exactly."

"Wait a minute," Matt grumbled. "First you tell us you found something, and now you say you didn't. Which is it?"

"There's NO Smitty's in this town."

"There isn't? But then..." Jimmy started thinking.

"Are you telling us it's a fake?"

"Yes."

"But why? I mean, who would go around with a truck that had a phony name on it?"

"Suppose they wanted everyone in the neighborhoods to *think* they were from a real place?" Tom asked.

Matt laughed. "I saw this show on TV last week where a reporter rode around all night with this guy who went out and picked up cars from people who'd stopped paying the bank."

"The repo guy. Yeah, I saw that too," Jimmy added. "Could it be something like that?"

Tom thought for a moment. "I'm not sure. Like I've said before, we need to keep our eyes open."

"Speaking of eyes open, we'd better get home," Matt suggested. "Cause if I don't get my eyes closed pretty soon, they won't be open on our route."

All agreed they would think of ideas to help solve the mystery. Early the next morning, Tom's friends arrived, right on time. He liked the way his paper route helped everyone become more disciplined about keeping on schedule. But again Tom found himself lost in another article about the thefts.

"Essentially," the article began, "authorities say the racket works like this: a body shop calls the junkyard to place an order for specific parts off of a particular car. The junkyard calls the thieves, who find the exact make and model of the car required. The car is stolen and taken to another location where it is torn apart, piece-by-piece. The chop shop..."

Tom looked up and exclaimed, "Chop shop!"

Matt and Jimmy stopped working. "You reading again?" Matt complained.

"Listen to this. A junkyard owner had guys go out and steal cars so he could cut them up and sell the parts for thousands and thousands of dollars."

"That's what my uncle said about cars being worth more in pieces than all together," Jimmy reminded his friends.

"After we finish our route today, I'm going to do some more investigating," Tom announced.

"Well, if you don't start rolling papers we're gonna be late," Matt threatened.

Tom began getting his stack of papers ready, but he couldn't get the article out of his mind. Even as the boys began their deliveries, Tom's friends had to remind him about where to throw his papers. That was after the first two landed in a fountain.

"Fish don't like to read," Jimmy joked, "even if they do swim in schools."

When they made the turn onto Deer Path Lane, Tom

stopped his bike. It was still dark out causing Matt and Jimmy to almost plow right into him.

"What are you doing?" Jimmy asked.

"Shhh. I think I saw something." Tom dropped his bike to the grass and hurried into a row of bushes. Matt and Jimmy followed close behind. When they reached Tom, the boys looked across into an empty parking lot of a fast food place. A man stepped out of an expensive looking car. He had a plastic bag in his hands. First, he looked around to be sure no one was watching. Then he walked to one of the large trash containers, looked around again, and stuffed the bag into the trash.

"What's the big deal?" Jimmy asked. "It looks like a guy throwing out his garbage."

"At this time of morning?" Tom whispered. "And besides, look at the way he's dressed, and that car. I think he can afford his own trash cans at home."

The man looked around one last time, then hurried back to his car. He slipped behind the wheel, slammed his door, and drove off.

"This is way too exciting for me," Matt teased.

"I guess you're right. I don't know what I was thinking," Tom said. They stood to their feet, turned, and took three steps in the direction where they'd left their bikes when something unusual happened.

"Get down," Tom whispered. "Someone's coming."

He turned around again and crouched behind the same bushes. As Matt and Jimmy joined him, another car drove into the parking lot. The restaurant wasn't open yet so all the lights were still off. The car's lights went out when it came to a stop in front of the trashcan they had just seen.

The boys watched in amazement as a woman got out of her car, walked to the trash container, reached in, and pulled out the same plastic bag.

"Now I've seen everything," Matt whispered.

The woman returned to her car. As she sat behind the wheel, they could see her from the light inside. She opened the bag, reached in, and pulled out a hand full of cash. Then she looked around the parking lot, put another hand in the bag and pulled out more money. She glanced up and started laughing wildly. A minute later she started her car, turned on the lights, and drove away.

"Let's get out of here!" Jimmy yelled.

But as they were about to run, the boys heard a low, frightening growl.

Matt shuddered. "Maybe if we don't turn around it'll go away."

Slowly they began to move. As they did Tom noticed that the dog from Maple Street doesn't always *stay* on Maple Street.

"Anybody got your spray?" Tom asked. No one made a sound. The dog moved a little closer, and then stopped.

"We have to show him we aren't afraid," Matt told them. "That's what my uncle said."

Jimmy quivered. "You go ahead and show him if you want to because I'd be lying."

"Let's take a step toward him and see what happens," Tom suggested.

Up until this time the boys had been standing in complete darkness. As they stepped forward they moved into the beam coming from a nearby streetlight. When they did that, the dog took a step back.

"I think it's working," Matt said. So they took another step and this time they were standing completely in the light. Now the dog could see exactly who they were. He relaxed from his attack position, stopped snarling, and began wagging his tail. Next he did something odd. He trotted up to Matt and pushed his nose against his leg. Then he started whining.

"Hey Matt," Jimmy called out. "I think you've trained him."

"We gotta go now," Matt said, and the three ran off.

They hurried back to their bikes and rode away, trying to pretend they hadn't seen what just happened in the parking lot, but it was hard to ignore.

When the boys returned to Tom's house, after delivering the rest of the papers, they went straight to the garage.

"Tom?" Matt asked. "Do you think those trash bag people have anything to do with all the stolen cars?"

"How should I know?"

"Aren't you supposed to be the great detective?" Jimmy mocked.

"He's a defective detective," Matt teased.

"It's one of the strangest things I've ever seen, but right now I don't know what to think about it. Listen, I'm going to go back to the library. I'll call you guys later."

"What for?" Matt asked.

"I've got an idea," Tom told them.

Chapter 6

Tom hurried on his bike toward the library. He parked in the rack, like before, and walked to the doors. But when he pulled on the handle, the door didn't open. He pulled even harder, but it seemed to be stuck. Then he looked at his watch.

"Eight forty-five," he said.

A little old lady sat on a bench not far from the entrance. She looked up and added in a squeaky voice, "That's right. They don't open until nine. I like to come down early and feed the pigeons while I wait."

"I've never seen you here before," Tom remarked.

"I don't come every day. Since I have to ride the bus, it's not as easy as when I had my car."

"What happened to it?" Tom asked.

The woman sat up straight. "Someone stole it."

Suddenly, Tom became interested in talking with her. "When did it happen?"

"About two weeks ago."

"Did you report it to the police?"

"I sure did. And do you know what they told me?"

"What?"

"They said it was my own fault for parking it in my driveway."

"What's wrong with that?"

After a short, embarrassed giggle she said, "I didn't lock it."

"Oh. That's one of the first rules about keeping crooks from stealing your car. I read it in a book."

"I know that now, but it was right beside my own house. And that isn't the worst of it."

"What do you mean?" Tom asked.

"Not three days before that, I had just spent three hundred and fifty dollars to have it repaired."

Tom slid a little closer to her on the bench. "Do you mind telling me where you had it fixed?"

The woman reached into her purse and took out a yellow piece of paper. She handed it to Tom. When he unfolded it he could hardly believe what he saw.

"P. J.'s Auto Repair," he whispered. "Listen," he continued, "could I borrow this for a couple days?"

"Whatever for?"

"Well, actually, I'm a paper boy. You might not believe this, but I'm trying to figure out who's stealing all the cars around town."

"Isn't that what the police are supposed to be doing?" she asked.

"Yes. And I know they're trying. But I've seen some pretty strange things happening along my route. My friends have too. We think the police might not be looking in the right place, that's all."

"I don't know," she hesitated.

"Look. This bill has your name and address on it. It also shows what kind of car you have ... I mean had. It would really help if I could hold on to it a little longer. I promise I'll bring it back to your house when I'm finished."

"I guess that would be all right," she sighed. "The loveliest little white Buick you ever saw. The license says 'PRINCESS.' My Harold did that too" Her little voice trailed off into memories. "He always called me his princess..."

Just then Tom heard the lock open on the library door. "I gotta find something," he called over his shoulder as he opened the door. He quickly returned to the reference section. The woman who had helped him find the city directory was on duty again this morning.

"My, my. Back so soon?" she asked with a smile. "You must like it here."

"A guy can learn a lot from a library," Tom answered.

"I wish more smart boys your age knew that," the woman sighed. "So, what will it be this time?"

"I need a map of the city."

"We have several different kinds. What are you looking for, exactly?"

"Something with all the streets on it. Mostly where people live."

"So you're interested in residential, not so much the downtown area?"

"Right."

She stood up and walked over to a cabinet with large drawers. From one she pulled out an oversized binder. After flipping through several pages she announced, "Here. This should do the trick."

Tom came closer, but the map looked confusing. "How do you make sense out of it?" he asked.

The woman pointed along the top of the map. "See these numbers?"

"Yes."

"And these letters along the side?"

"Uh huh."

"Then on the back you can find the name of the street you need. They're in alphabetical order. Each street has a letter and number after it. All you have to do is find those coordinates on the map."

"Coordinates?"

"You draw two imaginary lines. When they come together, you've found the spot."

"Oh. I see. Could you make a copy of both sides for me?"

"Yes, but it will be much smaller."

"That's okay," Tom agreed.

The woman took the map to another room. When she came back she handed a small copy to Tom. "That will be twenty-five cents."

Tom reached into his pocket, pulled out some change, and found a quarter. "Here, and thanks."

He headed back down the stairs and toward the doors. The old woman he had talked with earlier was sitting at a big, round table, reading the newspaper. Tom went over to see her again.

"You can subscribe to the paper," he told her. "Me and my friends bring it right to your door every day."

"I know. I used to take the paper. But now that my car is gone this is one of the few places I can go, just to get out of the house for a few hours."

Tom noticed a sad look on her face. "If I ever see your car, I'll be sure to let you know."

"I doubt you will," she sighed. "My husband bought me that car, not long before he died. He was so proud of it because he knew how happy it made me feel. Now that he's gone, the car meant everything to me." She reached up and brushed a small tear from her cheek. "I just know Agnes is gone for good."

"Agnes? Your husband's name was ... Agnes?"

"No. That was my car's name."

"You named your car, Agnes?"

"Why of course. Doesn't everybody give names to their cars?"

"Listen," Tom interrupted. "I have to get going, but I hope you find your ... Agnes."

"Me too. I surely do."

Tom hurried home as fast as he could. He felt his idea would be the key to catching the people who were stealing all those cars. Back in his room he took out a copy of the newspaper story that listed the addresses where cars were missing.

His map not only showed the names of all the streets, the blocks were numbered too. That way he could find where the seven hundred block was on one street, or the three hundred block on another. He was pretty sure he'd be able to mark almost the exact spot for each house listed in the article.

He cleared a space on his desk so he could lay everything out. But then the phone rang.

"Hello."

"Hi, Tom."

"Hey, Jimmy. What's up?"

"Nothing, really. I just tried to call you earlier and there was no answer. Where were you?"

"The library. Remember?"

"Oh, yeah. Anyway, I need to pick up a new reflector for my bike. Do you want to go to the hardware store with me?"

"Sure. I need to fix one of my mirrors too," Tom remembered.

"When do you want to go?" his friend asked.

"I'm working on something right now. I'll call you later. Okay?"

"Sure. I'm not going anywhere."

"Okay, later."

"Later yourself," Jimmy answered.

Tom hung up the phone and went to work. First he made a list of all the streets mentioned in the newspaper. He put them in alphabetical order so they would be in the same order as the streets listed on the back of his map.

Thirty-five addresses, he thought. *That's a lot of cars.* He continued working for about an hour, matching up addresses from the article to places on the map. Then he came to the name Constance Willard. The address looked familiar.

Is that one of my customers? he wondered. Tom took the repair bill from his pocket. "It's her," he said. He added her place to his list and underlined it. Then he plotted the address on his map.

When he finished marking a red dot on the map for

each address, Tom noticed the strangest thing.

Chapter 7

Tom was ready to meet Jimmy at the hardware store, but there was one more piece of the puzzle he needed. After dialing his friend's number he heard,

"Hi, this is Jimmy Wilson. Jimmy would like to talk with you, so if you'll leave your name and number, Jimmy will call you right back." Then Tom heard a tone.

"Hey Jim, this is Tom. I didn't know you had an answering machine. Anyway, I'm ready to go get those things we needed. Let me know when you're ready."

He was about to hang up when a voice said, "I'm ready now."

"What?"

"I said I'm ready now."

"Did you just get home?" Tom asked.

"No, I've been here the whole time."

"When did you get the machine?"

"I don't have an answering machine. I just like to do

that once in awhile when people call. It really makes the telemarketers mad. I like that."

"So are you ready?" Tom asked.

"Sure."

"Oh. One more thing. Could you give me the address for your uncle's shop?"

"I think I have it on a pencil around here someplace. Why?"

"It's just a hunch."

"Here it is. 315 Elm."

"Okay, thanks. See you at the store." Tom checked the address on his map. When he found the spot, he made a large blue X. *Interesting*, he thought.

A few minutes later the boys met in the bike parts aisle of the store. Jimmy had already found what he was looking for. Now all Tom needed to do was find a bracket for his mirror.

"Could you tell me where to find one of these?" he asked an employee. Tom held out a rusted metal band that had broken.

"Go to the end of isle five. It's right next to the key-making machine. You can't miss it."

"Thanks," Tom said. He and Jimmy walked off to find the part. When they came to the end of the aisle, Tom began sorting through a basket with several sizes of the part he wanted.

"They must make these things for all kinds of stuff," he sighed. Just as he found a piece exactly like the one he held in his hand, he noticed something. A man stood with his back to Tom. Another store employee was busy making a copy of a key.

"Hurry up, will ya?" the customer demanded.

"I'm doing the best I can."

"Well I have to get back to the shop before anyone notices."

"You'll get your key. Just hold your horses."

"Don't tell me what to do," the customer demanded. "I can take my business someplace else you know."

"You do that, and I'll tell the cops," the employee threatened.

"Like fun you will. You're in this just as deep as the rest of us."

"Oh yeah? Then how come I don't make as much money as you do?"

"Because you just make the keys. I'm the guy who has to go out and..." The customer realized he was talking in a loud voice so he could be heard over the sound of the key-making machine. He quickly looked around to see if anyone was nearby. Tom and Jimmy crouched down even lower behind the shelf where they were hiding.

"We'd better get out of here," Jimmy whispered.

As the boys turned to go, Tom saw the nametag on

the customer's light blue shirt. "Jake," he whispered.

"Who's Jake?" Jimmy asked. Unfortunately, he said the name, Jake, just after the machine stopped. Anyone within fifty feet could hear him too, and the man in the uniform was a lot closer than that. He walked to the end of the isle where the boys hid.

"Run!" Tom yelled. They tossed the things they were planning to buy onto the nearest shelf and ran for the exit.

"Stop those boys!" Jake warned. But they made it out the front door, grabbed their bikes, and sped away. A few blocks later Jimmy called to Tom, "Hey, wait up." Tom slowed his bike to a stop. "How come we had to run for it?" Jimmy asked.

"I can't tell you right now. Not without Matt here."

"Tell me what?"

"I think I've figured out who's stealing the cars."

"How do you know for sure?"

"I don't, but the three of us are about to find out. Come on over to my house. We'll call Matt. Then I can lay it all out for you."

Before long the boys were up in Tom's room. He put the map up on his bulletin board like an army general, just before a big battle. "I want to tell you guys what I've found," Tom began. "And Jimmy ... you aren't going to like part of it."

"Are you going to try to blame my uncle again?"

"No, but you're close."

"I warned you about that," Jimmy threatened.

"Just hear me out. That's all I ask."

"So?"

"All these red marks are the places with missing cars."

"Couldja tell me what's going on because I don't get it," Matt complained.

"Here's what I think," Tom continued. He drew a large circle around the area where most of his red marks had been made. "Only a few cars were taken from places outside this circle. Tom pointed to the large blue X on his map nearly in the center of the red dots. "This is where your uncle's shop is."

"What are you saying?" Jimmy asked.

"It didn't make sense to me that they'd take the chance of that Smitty's truck being spotted, hauling a bunch of cars across town. Sooner or later, someone would have noticed. We did."

"You mean like the police or something?" Matt asked.

"Exactly."

"So, what then?" Jimmy demanded.

Tom hesitated for a moment. "There were a couple things I didn't tell you guys."

"Like what?"

"Remember the night we first saw the tow truck?"

Matt shuddered. "Who could forget?"

"Well, that night, there was a second man in the truck."

"There was?" Jimmy asked. "I never saw him."

"Me neither," Matt added.

"Well there was. And I saw him."

Jimmy blurted out, "I still don't see..."

But Tom interrupted, "I saw the name on his shirt. Then later when we were in your uncle's shop, I saw the same man."

"Well he could have been having his car fixed," Jimmy protested.

"No. I'm sorry, but he works there."

"Howdya know that?" Matt asked.

"Because he had on a light blue shirt and dark blue pants like all the other mechanics. That's how."

"But it doesn't prove anything," Jimmy said.

"No, not at first it didn't. But today, in the hardware store..."

"That was him?" Jimmy asked.

"Yes, and I saw the name on his shirt again."

"Jake?" Jimmy whispered.

"Jake," Tom answered. "And I think he's been watching out for the best kinds of cars to steal. It makes sense that people from close around the shop would want to have their work done there."

"Wait a minute," Matt said. "You think this Jake guy has been making keys for all these cars? But why?"

"Because then later he could walk up to any one of them, right in front of the owner's house if he wanted to. His new copy would open it just like the real key. All he has to do is unlock the door, hop in, start it up, and he's gone."

"But how can we prove any of this?" Jimmy asked.

"Well, after I studied the map a little more I noticed that Matt's house isn't far from most of the stolen car addresses."

"That gives me a creepy feeling," Matt groaned.

"I thought we could all spend the night at your house," Tom continued. "That way no one would suspect that we're on to something. We can slip out after dark and see if anything happens."

Jimmy smiled. "That's a great idea. Then we can prove that my uncle doesn't have anything to do with this. You'll see."

"I never said he did," Tom added. "I only said something didn't seem right. So let's plan on tomorrow night. Will that be okay with your mom, Matt?"

"Should be. She likes you guys probably more than I do."

"Great. And I'll bring my map too. Matt, doesn't your dad have an extra cell phone?"

"Yes."

"Think you could borrow it, just for the night?"

"No problem."

"Let's bring our air horns and dog spray too."

"What for?" Jimmy asked.

"Because you can't be careful enough if you plan to go out at night like we do."

The boys were excited about the possibility they might be the ones to crack this case. Tom especially wanted to help the nice lady he'd met. He didn't like it that someone could hurt such a sweet old lady like that. In fact, it made him angry.

Friday night soon came. Tom had arranged for the papers to be delivered in front of Matt's house Saturday morning. That way they could get going on their route right away without having to go all the way back to his house first.

Matt's father cooked out cheeseburgers. His mother made potato salad, Jell-O, and a rhubarb dessert. The boys ate until their stomachs had no more room. They didn't tell Matt's parents about the plan. They set up sleeping bags on the screened porch and settled in for what looked like a normal night of sleep. Then Matt's parents turned out all the lights in the house and went upstairs to bed.

Tom reached over to pull his backpack closer. "I brought a flashlight and these road flares too."

"Road flares. How come?" Matt asked.

"Who knows? They were in the garage so I threw them in my bag. You guys ready to head out?"

"Why not?" Matt answered.

It was already ten forty-five as they quietly opened the screen door and slipped out into the dark. The warm night air felt good, and the moon made it bright enough to see. Along with the streetlights, Tom thought it didn't feel as late as it really was.

"Think we'll see anything, Tom?" Jimmy asked.

"Part of me hopes we do, and part hopes we don't."

"Where should we go first?" Matt wanted to know.

"I marked some places on my map. Just follow me."

In silence they rode for about fifteen blocks until Tom spotted a park he was looking for. "There," he pointed.

"There what?" Jimmy whispered.

"That park is almost in the center of a group of the dots on my map. From there we can watch in four directions at the same time."

"Good idea," Matt added.

They peddled to a clump of bushes where the boys hid their bikes. Then Tom motioned for his friends to join him by the slide. "I think we should each take one side of the park."

"But there are four sides and only three of us," Jimmy noted.

"I know. We'll just have to let one of them go. And besides, we can still see that side in the dark. If anybody drives past there we probably won't miss it."

The park had hedges in each corner making perfect hiding places for everyone. Tom pointed out two spots for his friends to hide, and then he found one for himself. When he looked at his watch it was already eleven. *Wonder if we'll see anything*, he thought.

Time seemed to come to a complete halt. Even though it was getting late there were still a few cars that drove through the streets where the boys kept watch. Suddenly, Tom heard something running toward him in the dark. *I hope Maple doesn't come over this far*, he thought.

Just then Jimmy slid in next to him like a baseball player in the majors. Completely out of breath he barely managed to squeak, "Smitty's. I just saw Smitty's."

"Where?" Tom demanded.

"Over there on the street we aren't watching."

"I didn't see anything," Tom said.

"I know, but I did. He had his lights off. I ran over to that side and I think they're getting ready to take a car."

"Where's Matt?"

"I already sent him over there to watch so I could get you."

"Let's go!" Tom exclaimed. Together they raced toward where their friend was hiding. As they ducked down behind the same hedge, Tom peered over the top just in time to see the door of the truck open. Once again the light revealed a second man inside.

"It's Jake," he whispered.

Chapter 8

Tom had been afraid a few times in his life. Like just before a big test, or when it was time for report cards. But he had never, ever been so scared as he was right now. Not only was it dark out, and the boys were all alone, but they were actually watching a car as it was about to be stolen. Worse than that, Tom knew one of the men. His heart began beating so fast, he had to sit on the ground for a moment.

"What's wrong with you?" Jimmy whispered.

"I'll be okay. Just give me a minute. I need to think of a plan."

"Wouldya hurry up," Matt said. "Because somebody's car's about to be hauled off to..."

"Get ready," Tom ordered.

The boys watched as Jake stepped out of the truck. He reached into his pocket and pulled out a key. He slipped it into the car's lock and tried to turn it. But the lock wouldn't open. He tried again, but it still didn't work.

"What's wrong?" the other man asked. "You do have the right key, don't you?"

"Of course it's the right key. I'm not an idiot." But the harder he tried the angrier the truck driver became.

He stormed out of the truck. "Here. Give me that," he demanded. Then the driver tried the key. He couldn't make it work either. So he walked around to the other side and tried that lock, but no luck.

"The guy at the hardware store must have made a mistake," Jake suggested. "I mean, we haven't had any trouble with all the others we've stolen."

That sent a cold feeling through Tom.

The driver threw the key on the ground and went to the back of his truck. He hooked something under the front end of the car. Then he walked back to the levers on his truck and began lifting the car's wheels off the ground.

The tow truck made a loud noise as the hooks continued lifting.

"I've got it," Tom announced.

"Got what?" Jimmy squeaked.

"When they get ready to leave, we'll run across the street so they know somebody saw them."

"I'm not runnin' anyplace," Matt protested.

"We'll be okay," Tom said. "It should happen so fast they won't know what happened. I just want to rattle them."

"I'm already rattled enough for all of us," Matt

complained.

"After we run, we have to hurry to our bikes. If we ride fast enough, we might be able to see where they take the car. Then we can tell the police."

"I don't need this much excitement," Matt said.

"Just be ready," Tom ordered.

He tapped his friends on the shoulder. "When I give the signal, you guys follow me."

As soon as the car was up in the air, the tow truck driver quickly jumped back in the cab, shifted into drive, and began pulling away from the curb.

"NOW," Tom ordered.

The boys streaked across the street just a few feet from the front of the truck. By this time its headlights were on. Tom and Jimmy made it across, but Matt, well, he had a problem. He wasn't as fast as his friends, but something else happened. Right in the middle of the street, Matt tripped and fell. The truck roared as it moved forward. The driver almost drove right over Matt, nearly crushing his body under the massive front wheels.

Tom turned back and looked in horror, thinking his friend was about to be squished to death. Somehow the driver was able to instantly move his foot from the gas peddle and jam on the brakes just in time to stop his truck only inches from Matt's head.

At that instant Matt looked up into the powerful

headlights. Tom could see Matt's reflection in the truck's bumper, but worst of all, the men in the truck got a clear look at Matt's face. There was no way he could ever feel safe, walking around town after that.

"Run, Matt, run!" Jimmy yelled. Tom watched as the driver turned his head from Matt and looked directly into his eyes. Tom felt like he was going to pass right out.

While all of this was going on, something else happened. When the truck skidded to a stop, the car behind it flew forward. It hit the back of the truck with so much force that the whole front of the car smashed in. The crash made such a loud sound that people from a couple of the houses nearby turned on their lights as they peered out of their windows.

Matt managed to get back to his feet and limped to the safety of the bushes on the other side. Once he was out of the way, the driver gunned it and rumbled down the street.

Then a man ran out from one of the houses. "Hey. Stop them. That's my car!"

"Let's get to our bikes," Tom called. "We can still catch them." He and Jimmy made it to the bikes at almost the same time, but Matt was a little slower. This time it was because his knee hurt from hitting the pavement. But he still ran pretty fast. The three boys jumped on their bikes and rode off in the direction of where the truck had gone.

Tom could still see its taillights in the distance as it turned onto another street.

"Come on, you guys. Hurry." Tom stopped quickly to pick up the key from the pavement. He put it in his pocket for evidence later.

"Matt. You still got your cell phone?" Tom asked.

Matt reached into his pocket but sadly reported, "I smashed it when I fell."

The boys peddled as fast as any racers they'd ever seen on TV. As they rounded the turn, Tom just caught a glimpse of the truck's lights again.

"There. I see them." And the chase was on again.

But the truck made a right turn onto one of the main roads in town. The speed limit was higher on that street. Tom knew there was no way they could ever keep up. He brought his bike to a stop.

"Hold it," he ordered.

His friends pulled up on each side.

"What do we do now?" Jimmy asked.

"There's nothin' we can do," Matt answered. "And my knee is killing me."

"Let's just go back to Matt's house. It's all over for tonight," Jimmy added.

"I guess you're right," Tom sighed.

The boys turned their bikes around when Tom saw it out of the corner of his eye.

"Wait just a minute!" he exclaimed.

The streetlights caused a reflection in something on the street. Tom hopped off his bike and knelt down beside a thin shiny stripe. He touched it with his finger, and then lifted it to his nose.

"Oil. The car is leaking oil," he announced. He turned his head in the direction where the truck had disappeared.

"Follow me!"

Again the boys began peddling like Olympic champions. All along their route, streetlights transformed the line of oil into a silver thread in the night. Now it didn't matter how fast the truck was going, Tom knew they could still find out where it went. The oil line only went straight for three blocks until it turned again onto a slower side-street.

"This way," Tom called.

"Hey," Jimmy yelled. "I hear something."

"It's a train," Matt said.

"Faster. Ride faster," Tom encouraged.

As they did, the boys were able to see the end of a freight train just as its last car rolled through the crossing and rumbled into the distance.

"There they are," Tom yelled.

As the crossing gate rose, the truck sped away.

Jimmy called out, "We got 'em now."

They wound through an area with dark abandoned

buildings. The street was rough, so the boys had to be extra careful not to get their bike tires stuck in the cracks and potholes all over the pavement. Tom noticed the truck couldn't go very fast either. He watched as it began making a left turn.

"Let's go down this alley," Tom pointed.

The alley went in the same direction as the street where the truck drove, but this way there was no possibility for the men to see them. It was only a hunch, but Tom thought they might be coming close to the place where the truck was about to drop off the car before heading out to steal another one.

He was right. When they came to the end of the alley, the boys looked down the street. They watched as the tow truck stopped in front of a high fence. Tom lowered his bike to the ground.

"Let's get closer."

The boys hid in the shadows as they made their way closer to the gate. In this part of town there were fewer streetlights. Plus, most of the buildings looked run down. Tom wondered how some of them kept from falling apart.

He heard the truck's horn as the boys stopped behind some rusty oil drums stacked near the fence.

The driver blasted his horn a second time, and something amazing happened. The gate began opening all by itself. Tom looked around to see if anyone was pulling on it, but they weren't. It reminded him of a big prison gate.

Tom motioned to his friends. "Come on."

They moved forward in a crouched position, making sure they stayed out of the light. The gate came to a stop, and the truck pulled inside the fence. Then the gate began to close.

"We're not going in there, Tom," Matt cried.

As the truck pulled up to a darkened building, a large door began to open, just like the gate. The truck moved forward and disappeared inside as the door closed again automatically.

Tom leaned against the fence. "We gotta see what's in there."

Suddenly the boys heard a low growling sound. Then another, and another. Tom looked up just as three mammoth guard dogs charged the fence. They slammed against it only inches from Tom's head. He quickly pulled his fingers out of the fence and jumped back as the dogs barked their warnings. Lights came on inside the building.

"Dogs," Matt cried. "Why did it have to be dogs?"

"We'd better move before those guys come out and catch us," Jimmy suggested.

"Yeah, and don't forget. They saw me," Matt reminded them as he pointed at his chest.

"All right," Tom whispered. "But we *are* going to find a way in that place."

"You crazy?" Matt asked.

Tom looked back toward the dogs. "We just *have* to."

Chapter 9

Quietly the boys found their bikes and headed back to Matt's house. They crept onto the porch and slid into their sleeping bags. Tom looked at his watch. "Only three hours till our papers come."

"I'm going to feel like I was hit by a truck," Matt yawned.

"That's not funny," Jimmy added. "You almost were."

"We have to find a way to get past those dogs," Tom whispered. "Does your uncle have any more tricks, Matt?"

"I think so. But couldya wait? We can talk about that tomorrow."

"Ha," Jimmy laughed. "It already *is* tomorrow."

That made Tom smile as he drifted off to sleep. But sleep didn't last long. He was awakened to the sound of the newspaper truck dropping off another load of bundles. He knew it was his job to get them out. So Tom quietly shook Jimmy.

"Time to get up."

"It can't be," Jimmy complained. "I just shut my eyes."

"I know, but our papers are here."

Matt rubbed his eyes and stretched. "What do you mean *our* papers? It's your route, and the way I feel right now, you can keep it. All of it." Then he rolled over and closed his eyes.

"Come on," Jimmy encouraged. "Remember. We're supposed to be like the mailman. Our papers have to get delivered no matter what the weather, or how we feel."

Tom thought for a moment. "Think of all those other guys who want to play center this fall. They're asleep right now too."

"You really know how to hurt a guy," Matt whined. Then he slipped out of his sleeping bag. "Tell me that's not rain I hear. You know how I hate those little plastic bags."

"It's rain all right," Tom told him.

"Then maybe I'll just try out for basketball. At least those guys have enough sense to play indoors."

"Matt," Jimmy reminded, "have you looked in the mirror lately? I mean, you're my friend and everything, but basketball?"

"I know. I know. Come on, those papers aren't going to run to their houses all by themselves."

"That's what I like to hear," Tom said.

Since they were at Matt's house, the boys had to drag

their papers onto the porch where they had spent the night. They spread them out on the floor, and then sat on their sleeping bags. Tom set up an assembly line. Matt rolled the papers while he and Jimmy slipped them into the plastic.

"This is going a lot faster than I thought," Matt said. Then he looked at the pile of rolled up papers next to Tom.

"Hey, you aren't doing your job," he complained. But Tom ignored him. Right then he was concentrating on another story in the paper.

"Listen to this. The mayor and chief of police are planning a news conference on the courthouse steps at eleven today."

"So?" Matt asked.

"So I'm going."

"Why? What's so important?" Jimmy asked.

"They're supposed to talk about their investigation into the stolen cars, that's what."

"You're gonna have to do this one without me," Matt told him. "I have to help my mom today."

"I'm out too," Jimmy added. "Today is clean the garage day at my house."

Tom gave his friends a disappointed look. "Then I guess it's up to me."

If it hadn't been for the rain, the deliveries would have gone smoothly. Except for the one corner Matt tried to take too fast. His bike slid out from under him scattering newspapers clear across the intersection.

"Good thing we used plastic bags," he said.

"I thought you hated those things," Tom commented.

"I wonder if the people sleeping in their beds appreciate what we do for them," Matt grumbled.

When they got back to Matt's house after their route, Tom asked, "Do you think your parents would mind if we stayed here again tonight?"

"I doubt it, but what about the papers tomorrow?"

"I'll call in again and set it up."

"Okay."

As Tom and Jimmy headed to their houses, Tom kept thinking about what they had seen the night before. It seemed like whenever there was a stolen car, Jake wasn't far away. Tom worried that Jimmy's uncle might get arrested and sent to jail.

A little before eleven he told his mother he needed to go out to check on something. Tom's parents trusted him and didn't question where he was going every time.

He sped off toward the courthouse. He was almost late. By the time he got there, a lot of people had already gathered. Tom saw television cameras, radio station microphones, and he even recognized a couple reporters from his own newspaper. Of course, reporters were far too important to notice someone who only delivered the paper.

Soon Tom watched several people coming out of the

courthouse as they moved toward a cluster of microphones. The TV people turned on their lights and started rolling tape.

"Good morning. I'm Mayor Aldrich for any of you who don't know me. Today we are gathering on the steps of the courthouse as a symbol of our determination to stop the car thefts in our city."

The sheriff spoke next. "We believe this is the work of people from outside the community. We think the cars are being transported out of the area."

I could tell him a few things, Tom thought.

The mayor came back to the microphones. "Joining me this morning are the sheriff, the chief of police, and a member of the FBI."

Tom sort of heard the comment about the FBI, but he also thought he saw something. Standing all the way on the other side of the crowd was someone who looked familiar. Tom edged through the mass of people, trying to get a better look. Then, for just an instant, he was positive, "Jake?" he whispered in disbelief.

How could someone be so brave that he'd steal cars one night and come to a news conference like this the next morning? he wondered. Just as Tom reached the place where he'd seen him, Jake ran to a nearby car, jumped in, and drove away.

Before Tom left, he scribbled "P. J's Auto Repair" on

a piece of paper and gave it to one of the reporters from his paper. Then he ran to his bike and rode off.

"I'm telling you it was him!" Tom exclaimed to his friends later that afternoon.

"Maybe it just looked like Jake," Jimmy suggested.

"Look. I saw him the first night. Then he turns up at the repair shop. Next we see him having a key made and talking about stealing cars. Last night he was there again and all three of us saw him try to use the key that didn't work. Now the news conference today. He has something to do with all of it."

Suddenly the boys heard the sounds of more sirens than ever before. They seemed to be swarming from all over.

"Quick. To the bikes!" Tom shouted.

They began riding in the direction where the sounds had gone. But when they came around the last corner, no one was prepared for what they saw. Especially Jimmy.

"It's your uncle's shop," Matt announced.

They came to a stop about half a block away. A police car blocked the street as officers stretched yellow tape to keep people back.

Jimmy looked on in horror as his uncle came out in handcuffs. "I can't believe this," he cried.

"We need to talk," Tom told him.

"Talk about what?" Jimmy groaned.

"Just come with me."

The boys walked their bikes to a nearby park and sat together around an old army cannon in one corner.

"So what do we have to talk about?" Jimmy asked.

"I don't know how to say this, but I think I might have had something to do with your uncle getting arrested."

Jimmy didn't listen to another word. "Why you..." he yelled as he lunged at Tom, pushing him to the ground. "I told you not to say anything bad about my uncle."

Tom struggled to get up. "I didn't. Honest. It's that Jake character. I know he only works in your uncle's place, but I also know he's up to no good."

Matt helped to pull Jimmy off before he did something he'd be sorry for later.

"I have a plan," Tom continued as he brushed the dirt from his clothes. "And if I'm right, we can clear up everything, including your uncle."

"I'm listening."

"Matt," Tom began. "You said you had an idea for the dogs."

"That I do."

"What was it?"

"Well, my uncle told me how to make the dogs sleepy."

"What are we going to do, tell them a bedtime story?" Jimmy sneered.

Matt pulled something from his pocket. "First we

blow on this dog whistle. People can't hear it, but the dogs won't like the sound *at all*."

"Then what?" Tom asked.

"We have to buy a couple pounds of raw hamburger."

Tom pulled a wad of bills out of his pocket. "No problem."

"Along with the whistle, my uncle sent some stuff we can put in the meat that will make the dogs sleepy. He uses it sometimes in the movies. It doesn't hurt them, and before long, they wake up and don't know what happened."

"Cool," Tom said.

"He told me to be careful with it, and how to use the stuff. The dogs are about fifty pounds each, right, Tom?"

"About that."

"Let's get going," Jimmy begged. "My uncle is on his way to jail right now and that Jake is probably planning to steal another car."

Tom nodded his head. "Tonight, those dogs belong to *us*."

Chapter 10

The boys went to a nearby grocery store to buy the hamburger. Back at Matt's house they rolled it into meatballs, each the size of a baseball. Next Matt carefully measured out the sleep powder and poured it into a hole he made with a pencil. Then he closed up the hole and put each meatball into a large plastic sandwich bag.

"I hope this stuff works," Jimmy said.

That evening they had to wait until after dark. Matt's parents went to bed around ten.

"Okay," Tom whispered. "Let's go."

The boys crept off the porch, quietly found their bikes in the dark, and headed back toward the old warehouse as fast as they could.

"Think we'll see any stolen cars come in tonight?" Matt asked.

"I don't know," Tom answered. "But I do know we'll see some dogs."

Matt reached down and grabbed the bag filled with meatballs. He gave it a good shake. "I'm all ready for them," he growled.

The boys rode quietly the rest of the way. Soon they could see the tall fence again.

"I'm glad that fence is there," Matt said.

"How come?" Tom asked.

"Well, it sure keeps us out, but it keeps the dogs in."

"Yeah, only we need to get inside tonight and see what we can find out."

"Oh. Right. I almost forgot."

They brought their bikes to a silent stop not far from the gate.

"Are you ready, Matt?" Tom asked.

He took the silent dog whistle out of his pocket. "Ready and waiting," he smiled.

"Then blow your horn."

Matt began blowing on the whistle as long and hard as he could. In seconds they heard the faint sound of barking. Just as before, the vicious attack dogs stormed the fence. When they got there they began jumping up against it as if they wanted to come right through and tear the boys apart.

"Okay, Matt. Work your magic," Tom ordered.

Matt opened the plastic bag and let one of the dogs get a whiff of the raw meat. That one stopped jumping and squealed as if to say, "Give me some, okay, huh? Whadaya say? Just one little piece?"

Matt wound his arm up like a World Series pitcher and threw the first meatball over the fence. All three dogs charged off after it. They fought like ... well ... dogs. Quickly Matt threw the rest over near them, and just as quickly, they gulped them down.

"So far, so good," Tom whispered.

"Now what, Matt?" Jimmy asked.

"Now we just wait and see what happens."

"Let's hide over by those barrels again," Tom suggested. In the darkness they were able to watch the dogs and keep an eye on the gate at the same time. A few minutes later, the first dog sat on the ground and laid down. Then the second did the same thing. Soon all three were stretched out in the dirt.

"That's pretty funny looking," Jimmy laughed. "Looks like my dad, my uncle, and my grandpa in front of the TV after Sunday dinner."

"I don't think your family would like to hear you say they look like a pack of wild dogs," Matt whispered.

"Shhh," Tom cautioned. "I hear something." The boys turned in time to see two cars driving toward the gate with their lights off. "Now's our chance," he said.

"Chance for what?" Jimmy asked.

"To get inside."

"You nuts?" Matt demanded.

"Nobody said you had to come along."

"But we're friends. And friends should stick together," Jimmy said.

Matt folded his arms in defiance. "Then I say we stick together *outside* the fence."

Tom looked at Matt. "Do what you want. I'm going." Slowly, Jimmy and Tom moved toward the gate. The first car sounded its horn while the second one waited close behind. Just as it happened before with the tow truck, again the gate began to open.

"Once the cars pull in," Tom whispered, "we need to hurry through before the gate closes. And we have to do it without those drivers seeing us."

Fortunately it was dark out. There wasn't much chance the boys would be spotted by anyone. And since the dogs were asleep, everyone would be safe ... maybe.

Matt was the last one in the gate, squeezing through just as it was about to close. His shirt got caught on a sharp piece of metal sticking out from the latch, and it pulled him backward.

"Hey you guys. Help."

Tom and Jimmy hurried back to pull him loose as the gate slammed closed.

"We shouldn't be in here," Matt complained.

But Tom simply motioned for them to move forward. The large door to the building had already allowed the cars to pull in, and it was closed again.

"Now what?" Jimmy asked.

"Let's try to get a look inside through the windows," Tom suggested. Off to one side he saw another pile of barrels. The way they were stacked looked almost like a stairway. It led up to a row of windows. Tom saw a faint light shining through the glass. "This way," he whispered.

Soon all three boys were crouched next to the windows. As Tom rose up to peek through he noticed the glass was so dingy, it was impossible to see what was on the other side. Then he found one that had a corner broken out. With one eye he looked into the room.

"There's nothing in there," Tom reported.

"Whadaya mean, nothing?" Matt asked.

"They must have taken them farther inside, so no one could see them from the windows."

"These guys are pretty smart," Jimmy added.

"I think we should go around back," Tom suggested. Like commandos, they walked around the side of the building.

"It's so dark, I can't see a thing," Matt complained. Then all three slipped and fell into some kind of hole in the ground. But they didn't just fall. They began sliding and Tom felt himself going down, like on the slides in the park.

This must be one of those places where trucks pull in, he thought.

"Why is it so gooey?" Jimmy asked.

"Probably grease from all the cars," Tom answered. He was sure they were about to plow right into a big door, but they continued sliding. Finally they came to a stop in a dark room with just enough light that Tom could faintly see an outline of the walls.

"I think we're in a basement or something," he said.

"My mom is gonna be very upset," Matt complained. "She just bought me these new jeans."

"Well, we've come this far. Might as well finish what we started," Jimmy sighed.

They made their way across the room toward a door. Light spilled through the cracks so they walked carefully up to the metal steps. Tom tried the knob and found the door opened easily. He gave it a push so he and his friends could squeeze through.

"Nothin' here either," Matt said.

"We saw the cars come in, and they didn't come out," Tom reminded him. "They've gotta be in here someplace."

The boys continued walking down a long dark hallway until they thought they heard voices. It sounded to Tom like the people were arguing. When he and his friends came to the end of the hallway, it opened into a large room that was at least three stories tall inside. And the men *were* arguing.

"It's getting too dangerous," a tall man with dark

scruffy hair and an equally scruffy beard warned.

"You trying to chicken out?" a heavy man in a nice clean suit demanded.

"The cops are getting closer, that's all I know."

"Yeah," a third man said as he stepped from the shadows. "At the news conference they said the FBI was on the case now. And a few minutes ago, the owner of the car I ripped off almost smacked me with a garden rake."

"It's Jake," Tom whispered to his friends.

"Well," the man in the suit reminded them, "you both make good money for a few hours work. I don't want to have to tell my boss there are any problems. Understand?"

"I understand it's getting too hot in this town," the scruffy man complained. "I think it's time we moved on."

"Move on?" Jake snapped. "We've hardly started."

"Hardly started? *Hardly started*? Me and you have stolen over three hundred cars so far."

"Three hundred," Tom whispered. "Man."

Matt moved over to a spot so he could see better. But when he did, something terrible happened. He still had grease on the bottom of his shoes. His right foot slipped out from under him as he fell into a stack of empty paint cans. The crash made more noise than all the cans on the back of a "just married" car.

Immediately the men stopped talking and turned toward where the boys were hiding.

Tom looked over to Matt who just shrugged his shoulders.

"Who's there?" the man in the suit demanded. "This is private property. You're trespassing. Do you know that? I'll have you arrested."

That idea was so funny to Tom, before he could stop himself, he laughed right out loud. When the men heard him, they began coming toward the boys.

"Let's get out of here," Jimmy cried.

But before they moved, Tom took an air horn from his backpack. He quickly slapped a piece of duct tape over the trigger, setting off an ear-splitting blast. He set it on the floor while it continued to wail.

Together the boys headed back toward the side entrance where they'd come in. Because it was so dark, the men couldn't see them. Once outside Tom and his friends ran as fast as they could toward the fence. But before they got there, they heard something awful.

Sitting directly in front of them, were those three dogs, and they were no longer asleep. One of the dogs growled in a low, terrifying tone. All three boys skidded to a stop and stood perfectly still. Then, without warning, the dogs slumped to the ground again and just lay there like stuffed animals.

Suddenly a car roared out the big front door with its lights on bright.

"You guys make a run for it," Tom yelled. "I'll head off the goons." He watched as his friends raced to the fence. They hit it so hard that both climbed up and over the top in an instant.

"Bring back help!" Tom called to them as he ran back toward the building.

Chapter 11

Tom could only hope his friends would get back in time with the police. He was about to hide outside someplace when all three dogs woke up. This time they *were not* going back to sleep. Their legs looked a little wobbly, but they still managed to block the escape route he planned to take. So Tom turned and ran around the other side of the building.

"There he goes!" someone called out.

"Get him!" another voice commanded.

Tom found another door that wasn't locked. He pushed through it and moved back toward the great room. He heard a loud door slam along with the sound of feet running toward him.

There wasn't any time to think. Tom had to move quickly. As he went deeper into the room he couldn't believe what he saw. There were cars and car parts strewn all over the place. Off to one side sat a truck trailer with nothing but car engines strapped to it. It looked like they were about to be shipped out because each was sitting in a separate wooden crate. Tom scurried over to hide behind the giant wheels on that trailer.

Just as he slipped out of sight, the men ran into the room.

"There's no way out of this place," one of them threatened. "So you might as well come on out."

Tom didn't make a move or a sound.

"If you want, we can let the dogs in. We'll just leave, and when we come back, you'll be nothing more than..."

It didn't seem possible, but Tom's heart started pounding even harder. He knew from reading all the articles, the information about chop shops on the Internet, and the news conference with the FBI, that these men didn't care who they had to hurt. All they wanted was to steal cars and make money. No one and nothing was going to get in their way.

"I'm warning you," the man threatened again. "I'll count to ten. After that, it's up to the dogs."

"One!"

Tom looked around for a place to hide, or where he could go higher and away from the dogs. He saw a ladder leading up to a metal walkway going around the entire room. But it was clear across in the opposite corner.

They'll see me for sure, he thought. Tom wondered if

his friends made it to the police station by now because he was running out of ideas.

"Two!" the voice thundered.

Tom slipped from his hiding place under the trailer and moved to the other set of wheels nearer the wall. Then as he turned his head, he saw something.

"Three! I'm warning you."

Off in a distant corner sat a white car. *I wonder*, Tom thought. With all the boxes and car parts it would be easy for him to get closer to that car without anyone seeing him. Tom began to crawl away at first.

"Four!"

When he was a little farther out of sight, he stood up and moved quietly toward the car.

"Five. I'm halfway to ten!"

This guy is brilliant, Tom thought. *He knows his numbers ... all the way to ten.*

"Six!"

Now Tom was only a few feet from the car, but a tarp covered the front so he couldn't see the license plate. He crept a little closer.

"Seven!" the voice called from the distance.

Tom reached the car and lifted the tarp. *Of course,* he thought. *They took the plates off.* He eased around the side so he could peer in through the window. There was a lot of black dust on the glass. Tom wiped some of it off and looked inside.

"Eight!"

He didn't see anything on the front seat, but when he looked in the back, there on the floor was a plate. "If it only wasn't upside down," Tom whispered.

"Nine!"

Tom quietly opened the door, reached in, and pulled out one of the license plates. When he turned it over he read, PRINCESS. *That's it,* he determined. *The old woman's car.* A smile spread across Tom's face as he remembered how sadly she talked about losing that car. *It was almost like her best friend died,* he thought.

"This is your last chance," the voice called out.

The smile on Tom's face instantly changed to fear. Quietly he bowed his head and closed his eyes. "Lord," he prayed softly. "I know I probably shouldn't have come in here, and maybe we could talk about that later, because I'm *in* here now." He looked up for a moment to make sure he was still safe. "Please let my friends be okay so they can bring help soon. And thank you for how you promise to take care of us once we trust in Jesus. Amen." Tom looked up just as the man called out,

"TEN!"

He heard the men's voices again. It sounded like they were deciding what to do with him.

"Get the dogs," the man ordered. Tom raised up high

enough to watch the scruffy man hurry toward the doors.

"You can't kill him," Jake demanded.

That's odd, Tom thought. *Why would he care anything about me?*

"It isn't right," Jake continued

"Oh, I see. And stealing cars is?"

"That's different. With the cars, insurance companies pay up and the owners are happy. But with a kid ... I don't know."

Now Tom heard the dogs. They didn't seem to have as much energy as before, but they still sounded pretty angry to him. He decided that his only chance was to get on that ladder. Then he remembered something.

Flares, he thought. He reached into the small backpack he'd been wearing and pulled out three old flares his father had planned to take for disposal. Tom rescued them, but at the time he had no idea why he wanted to keep flares.

The instructions were almost rubbed off the sides, but he found a diagram. It showed that he needed to pull the top off. Then if he struck the two parts together, it was supposed to work.

When the dogs stormed in, something very strange happened. The man in the suit ordered one of them to go after Jake. That didn't make any sense to Tom. He watched as the dog chased him. Jake ran toward an office. The dog still looked kind of wobbly, Tom thought, because it didn't quite catch him.

If it hadn't been for the sleep stuff, he would have caught Jake for sure, Tom thought.

Jake rushed into the small office, slamming the door just in time. The dog stood outside, growling and scratching at the door.

Now the man ordered the other two dogs to find Tom. At first they ran toward another part of the room when suddenly one of them slid to a stop. He poked his nose in the air and started sniffing. Then he turned his head in the direction where Tom was hiding. The dog looked for a moment, then showed his teeth, and uttered an evil growl.

Tom pulled his flare apart. He wasn't sure what was going to happen, but he knew the men would find him if he hid in the car. And if he ran, one or the other of those ferocious dogs was sure to get him. At that moment the second dog also sniffed and turned in Tom's direction. Slowly they began advancing toward him.

Tom waited...and waited...and waited...until they were close enough that he could hear them breathing. Then both dogs stopped. Tom tried some of his pepper spray but the dogs were still too far away for it to do him any good. Their fiery eyes glared, as it seemed they now remembered exactly who Tom was.

Again they began creeping forward. In an instant

Tom struck the flare, but it didn't light. He tried again, but nothing. "Come on," he cried. The third time he struck the top of the flare, it burst into a red flame so blinding he had to turn away. He threw it like a grenade, right in front of the dogs. First they stopped. Then they backed up a little. So Tom lit another one and tossed it to one side of where the dogs stood. Quickly he struck his third and final flare. This one he tossed to the other side.

Now flaming flares on three sides and a wall directly behind them boxed in the dogs. In a flash, Tom darted past them toward the ladder clear across the room. He watched the dogs over his shoulder as he ran. As soon as they saw this, and even though the bright lights and smoke confused them a little, they found their way out of the inferno, and stormed off toward Tom.

He turned his head forward, running full speed toward the ladder. The dogs were so close now, Tom was sure he could feel their hot breath on his ankles. He tripped and nearly fell to the floor, but regained his balance and hurried on.

Almost there, he told himself.

He reached the bottom of the ladder just as the hairy monsters came skidding on all fours across the slick concrete floor. They crashed into the wall like bowling pins, but immediately jumped up again. That gave Tom the split seconds he needed to grab hold and begin his climb. Before he was in the clear, one of the dogs spun around, came to the bottom of the ladder and leaped into the air. He jumped so high he nearly bit Tom's leg. On the way back down he grabbed a shoelace between his sharp teeth. The force of the dog's weight as he fell back toward the floor snapped the lace, but Tom's shoe stayed on somehow.

Then both dogs continued leaping and barking at the base of the ladder. The third dog kept guard by the door where Jake was trapped, but the other two men had already left the building.

Tom continued climbing until he was all the way at the top, three stories high. At that moment he wasn't taking any chances of being caught. He sat on the walkway for a moment, and then decided he needed to get out of the building. Not only were the dogs after him, but by now, for sure, Jake knew exactly who he was. And there was always the possibility the building could burn down from the flares.

At the end of the walkway he noticed a small door. *Wonder where that goes,* he thought. Tom decided he couldn't stay where he was a minute longer, and began moving cautiously toward the door. When he reached it, and pushed the door open, he saw nothing but another ladder going back to the ground. The difference was, this ladder was on the other side of the doors from where the dogs were yelping. And he'd be away from Jake, too!

Tom started down the ladder, but with the grease

still on the bottom of his shoes, one of his feet slipped off the ladder. He hit his knee so hard it almost made him want to throw up. Dangling from the ladder, Tom held on as tight as he could until he was able to pull that foot back up and continue climbing down.

At the bottom he quickly started toward what looked like an exit. But before he could reach that door, he heard voices again. He dove into the middle of a stack of large cardboard boxes and did his best to stay out of sight.

A door opened and light spilled in, revealing Tom's hiding place. He pushed himself in as far as he could. The sound of footsteps stormed into the room. Silent shadows skimmed across the floor until one of them stopped, completely covering Tom's face. Tom reached up and covered his eyes. Silence had never sounded so loud as he waited to see what would happen next.

A thunderous voice commanded, "We know you're in there. Now come out with your hands up."

Tom stood to his feet, slowly raised his hands into the air, and began shuffling out from his hiding place. But when he did, he noticed all the men were standing with their backs to him.

Then in his bravest, most manly voice he cried, "Here...here I am."

Chapter 12

One of the men turned to see where Tom was standing. "Hey guys, look what we have here."

Tom stared past him and saw that the scruffy looking man and the man wearing the suit were over by the far wall in handcuffs.

"Wait a minute," Tom protested. "There's one more of them."

Jake stepped forward. "You mean me?"

"Yeah! Why aren't you wearing cuffs too?"

"Well, Tom. It's a long story."

"How come you know my name?"

"I know more than your name. In fact, I know all about you, and your friends, Matt and Jimmy."

"You do? But..."

Just as Jake was about to continue, three cages of very angry dogs were brought from the other room.

"Do you know what this place is, Tom?"

"I think it's a chop shop."

"You're right. It's one of the largest operations of its kind we've ever busted."

"But I thought..."

"I know. You thought I was in on it. And I know you tried your best to make sure before you told anyone. That was pretty smart. It gave us just enough time to complete our investigation. Just the same, you and the other boys nearly blew it for us tonight my friend."

"We're sorry."

"No need to be. It ended well. That's what matters."

"At first I was just excited about being the one who could solve the case. But then I met this sweet little lady. That's her white car in the corner of the big room."

The men went over and looked into the next room. Surprised, Jake looked back and asked, "How do you know it's hers?"

"Because she told me what kind to look for and the name on the license."

"The car still has its plates? Maybe these clowns aren't as smart as we thought."

"No, I saw both plates setting on the floor in the back seat. I think someone just forgot about them. But if I hadn't found them, how would anyone know whose car was whose?" Tom asked.

"Oh, I'm sure a lot of the evidence has already been

covered over, but these cars, and many of their parts, have identifying numbers. Since we were able to keep our operation a complete secret, except for you and your friends, there should still be a bunch of numbers that haven't been changed or scratched off yet.

"The main number is called a VIN. That means vehicle identification number," Jake continued. "Here, let me show you one." Tom looked through the windshield on one of the cars as Jake pointed to a number on the dash. He went on to show Tom numbers on some of the other parts. "You can find the VIN on things like the frame, the engine, and the transmission," Jake told him.

"I should put a number like that on my bike."

"That's not a bad idea. You could write your name or other information in a place no one would know to look. Then if it ever is stolen, and the police find it, you can prove it belongs to you."

Tom looked out across the room again. "I heard you guys say you'd stolen over three hundred cars. Is that true?"

"We think it's a little higher," Jake told him. "I didn't get involved until after they had their operation up and running. But because we were still able to surprise them, we'll be able to comb through their computer hard drives and find a lot more information about their customers, shipping addresses, and even identify the people higher on up the line."

"Well, then what do you do with all these parts. I mean, it's like Humpty Dumpty. You can't exactly put the cars back together again."

"That's true. And we know some of the best cars were shipped out of the country. For most of the owners, their cars are gone for good."

"But the ones that still are here? Like the white Buick in the corner?" Tom asked.

"We'll do our best to locate the owners. We compare our stolen car reports to the cars setting here. A few people are going to be mighty lucky, I can tell you that."

"And the lady that owns the Buick?"

"Don't worry. We'll find her."

"I already did. I know right where she lives."

"Well," Jake said, "make sure to tell one of the officers what you know. He'll see she gets her car back."

Tom smiled. "Thank you. I know she'll be real happy."

Just then Jimmy's uncle walked into the room.

"Hey," Tom said, "I thought you were in jail."

"No, I just had to make it look like I'd been arrested."

"Why?"

"So others in the gang would think they were safe ...and to take the heat off my friend Jake here."

"Your friend? I don't get it. You knew about him?"

"Sure did. Now I'm here to help with an inventory of all this stuff," he groaned.

Two firemen walked back to where the flares had been set off and made sure they were out with fire extinguishers. There was a lot of smoke, but most of it went up to the high ceiling.

"Hey, Tom!" a voice called out.

Tom turned to see Matt and Jimmy coming across the room.

"Did you catch those crooks all by yourself?" Matt asked.

Tom's face turned bright red. "I didn't catch them at all. Shoot, I almost didn't make it out alive. Those creeps turned the dogs loose on me."

"I thought they were still asleep," Jimmy said.

"Well, they woke up."

"Yeah," Matt added. "My uncle told me the stuff wears off pretty fast."

"I sure wish somebody would have told me that. One of them tried to bite my leg off."

A police officer told Tom, "If it hadn't been for your two friends here, there's no telling what might have happened to you."

"Thanks, guys," Tom said.

"They came flying into the station like the entire city was about to blow. At first we didn't believe their story until your friend, Matt ... well, let's just say he convinced us."

"I had to," Matt told him.

"Had to?" Tom asked.

"Sure."

"How come?"

"Who else was gonna play quarterback?"

The scruffy man and the man in the nice suit were taken outside toward a waiting police car with its lights still flashing. Tom watched as men with FBI on their jackets started carrying computers and files out of the office.

"Can I get a picture of the boys?" a man asked. Tom knew he worked for the newspaper, the very paper he and his friends delivered every day.

Tom, Matt, and Jimmy stood in front of a stack of car parts as the photographer fired off a bunch of pictures.

Jimmy grinned. "We are going to be *so* famous."

Tom walked over to where Jake stood writing some numbers on a clipboard. "I'm sorry I thought you were helping the crooks."

Jake looked up. "Not at all, Tom. Actually, I think you did some pretty fine detective work."

"I did?"

"Sure did. You noticed me in the truck on that first night. I saw you looking at me."

"No kidding?"

Jake nodded his head. "And again, back at the shop."

"Did you know we heard you in the hardware store?"

Tom asked.

"Yes. Then I saw you watching me at the news conference. All in all, excellent police work in my opinion."

"Police work, huh?"

"Some of the best I've ever seen."

Tom thought for a moment. "Are you going to stay here in town after this?"

"Wish I could, but there are more places, just like this, all over the country. Soon as we shut one down, it seems like five more pop up. And with the internet now, people can buy and sell parts, or even whole cars. It makes it more difficult for us to track them."

"One more picture over here," the photographer asked.

"Are we going to be in the paper tomorrow?" Jimmy asked.

"Son, in the morning, you boys are practically going to be the *entire* paper."

"Oh, man. I was hoping I could tell my parents first."

"By this time tomorrow, they'll know. Believe me, the whole town will know."

Chapter 13

Back at Matt's house, the boys again crept quietly onto the porch and slipped into their sleeping bags for another very short night. None of them was quite ready to go to sleep yet.

"What do you think our parents are going to say about all this?" Jimmy asked.

"Oh, I think we'll have a lot of explaining to do," Tom answered.

"Still ... pretty exciting. Don't you think?" Matt said.

Tom let out a long breath. "I'm still wondering what would have happened if you guys didn't make it to the police station in time."

"Are you kidding?" Matt asked. "You were the one who made it so me and Jim could get away. If you hadn't done that, I don't know."

"And on top of that," Jimmy added, "we're supposed to be friends. Friends to the end. Isn't that what we've always said?"

"I just did the first thing that popped into my head," Tom told them. "I'm glad it worked out, that's all." Tom silently prayed, thanking God that he was safe. He was also thankful for his two good friends.

After talking a little longer, the boys went to sleep. But in the morning, they were still sleeping so soundly, no one heard the delivery truck. No one, that is, except for Matt's parents.

"Matt," his father called from the kitchen. "Matt!" The boys sort of heard him, but it seemed like another bad dream to Tom until Matt's father came out onto the porch.

"You boys had better get up. Your deliveries are going to be late as it is."

Tom rubbed his eyes, and then looked at his watch. "Five-thirty. We're gonna be in such trouble," he cried.

The boys quickly dressed and hurried to the street. But when they got to the end of the driveway, there wasn't one stack of newspapers anywhere.

"How do you like that," Matt complained. "Can you believe someone came by and stole all your papers, Tom?"

"That can't be it. I'll call my supervisor. Can I use your phone?"

"Sure go ahead," Matt said.

The boys ran to the back door and into the kitchen. Tom took a card out of his pocket and dialed the number.

"Hello, this is Brian."

"Yes, sir. This is Tom. Tom Stevens."

"Good morning, Tom. I expected you to sleep in a bit longer this morning."

"You're kidding, right?"

"No. I'm not."

"Let me put it this way. Have you seen today's paper yet?"

"Actually, that's why I'm calling you, I haven't seen any papers here. You didn't take them to my house did you? Because I called and everything."

"Tom, you'll be happy to know your papers have already been delivered. If you look on Matt's front steps, there's a little surprise for you boys."

But while Tom was talking to his supervisor, Matt's father went to the front door looking for his own paper. Just then he walked back into the room with the strangest look in his eyes. "You boys had better come out to the front steps because you wouldn't believe it even if I told you what's out there."

The boys dashed to the front door and out onto the porch. Three copies of the morning paper had been lined up in a row. Each copy had a bright red bow tied around it, and one of the boy's names on each. There next to the papers were three new footballs, still in their boxes. But what was parked out in the front yard surprised them the most.

121

There, on the grass the boys saw three brand new bikes. Each one had a card taped to the seat,

"We didn't even see these in the dark," Tom shouted. "I was too upset that my papers hadn't come."

Tom found his bike and opened the card.

"Tom, please accept these gifts as our way of saying thank you for your good work. Not only are you one of the best carriers, but we think you did an outstanding job of noticing what goes on in the neighborhoods you serve. We pride ourselves in knowing that our carriers are alert to any problems along their routes that don't look right. But what you and your friends did went beyond anything the newspaper staff has ever seen before. So, enjoy the day off. Your papers have already been delivered for you. By the time you read this, all of your customers will be as proud of you as we are here at the paper. Mr. Davidson opened up his shop special so we were able to get the footballs and new bikes.

Tom could hardly belive what he read. But that was before he looked at the copy of the newspaper. Matt's father picked up his morning paper, which he found in the bushes, and opened it to the front page. "Would you boys like to explain any of this to me?" he asked.

After taking one look at the oversized picture of himself, Jimmy, and Matt, Tom could hardly make the words come out. "I wouldn't know where to start," he managed to say.

"Tom," Jimmy called. "Didn't you have a blue slip of paper in your card like the ones in ours?"

"Blue slip? What blue slip?" He walked back to his new bike and noticed a piece of paper that had fallen to the ground. Tom picked it up and read, *"Please come to the newspaper today at noon for a special presentation. Bring your family with you."*

"What's that about?" Matt asked.

"Search me," Tom answered. "Guess we'll have to wait and see. I have to get home. I'm sure my parents have read their paper by now."

"Me too," Jimmy added.

"Wait a minute," Tom said. "I can't ride two bikes home."

Matt's father said, "Leave your old ones here. I'll hold on to them until you can both come back later."

"Thanks Mr. Woodridge," Tom called over his shoulder as he ran for his new bike. He began speeding down the street without thinking about all the ribbons in the spokes on both wheels. Large red bows decorated each handle grip, with other streamers flapping in the wind.

I hope none of the other guys from school see this, Tom thought. *They'd never let me play quarterback after that.*

When he reached his driveway, Tom saw that every light in the house was on. He walked cautiously in the back door just as the phone rang.

"It's been doing that non-stop since five-thirty," his mother told him. "Everyone wants to talk to our hero."

"So I guess that means you've seen the paper?"

"Yes, and we're very proud of you, son," his father told him.

"You are? But..."

"The only thing I don't understand is why you didn't call the police earlier?"

Tom took a deep breath. "I thought about doing that but Buster told me I'd better be sure before I went off accusing people of a crime. Then everything started happening so fast."

"I'm sure there is a lot more to the story. And you can tell us about it when you're ready. Right now it seems like the whole town is grateful for what you did."

"It could have turned out real bad for me, Dad."

"I know. The story makes the whole thing sound pretty hair raising to me."

"Is it true there were attack dogs like they say here?" his mother asked, holding the paper in her shaking hands.

"Three of them."

"Thomas!" she scolded. "You really must be more careful."

"Once I knew the mess I was in, I asked God to help me, and I believe He did."

"I'm glad to hear that," his father complimented. "But

remember, God isn't there just for emergencies. He wants to guide us every step of the way, not only when we get ourselves into trouble."

"I know, but I didn't do it for me," Tom told them. "I met this nice lady. Her car had been stolen from right outside her house. It was the last present her husband gave her before he died. And those guys came along and took it. I can't explain it, but something just went off inside me and kind of took over after that."

Tom's parents continued listening.

"And you know what's the best part?"

His parents shook their heads.

"I found her car before they could cut it to pieces." Tears welled up in his eyes, and his voice cracked a little as he told his parents, "She's going to be so happy when she finds out. I'd like to go see her later today."

Tom's parents moved closer to him so they could give him a long hug. Right then Tom thought there couldn't be a happier twelve-year-old boy on the whole planet.

"The newspaper wants us to come down for something at noon today."

"The whole family?" his mother asked.

Tom nodded his head.

His mother got very excited. "Oh my," she giggled.

Chapter 14

Jimmy's dad owned a van big enough to take all three families down to the newspaper office. He and Matt came over to Tom's house early so they could talk.

"I'm glad we're all going together," Tom told them.

"Me too," Matt added. "Our car is such a junker. My dad says if it had new shocks, new tires, and new brakes, it still wouldn't start."

"He needs to see my uncle," Jimmy chuckled.

A few minutes later Jimmy's parents pulled up in front of Tom's house. Matt's parents were already in the van too. Tom ran to his front door and told his parents it was time to leave. On the way downtown, the boys and their parents tried to catch up on all the details.

"So," Matt's father began. "What exactly is going to happen when we get there?"

"Nobody knows," Tom told him. "All we do know is what our notes said."

When they drove into the parking lot in front of the newspaper office, a guard directed them to a special parking spot next to the doors. It had a big sign that said VIP.

"Who's Vip?" Matt asked.

"It stands for very important person," his father told him. "That's what they think of you boys. The rest of us are just along for the ride."

Everyone got out of the van. That's when Tom noticed a red carpet stretching from the front steps right up to their parking space. "I've never seen that before," he said. When they reached the top step, someone opened the front door so they could walk right in.

A crowd of people clapped, shouted, and whistled as the boys entered the lobby. Now Tom began feeling a little embarrassed. His supervisor introduced himself to the parents and then took the boys up front where three chairs were waiting. Tom noticed that some of the same people who had been at the news conference in front of the courthouse were also here including television and radio stations.

First the mayor stood up and made a speech. Then he read to the boys a proclamation from the city naming this Newspaper Carrier Day. Another man handed each boy a framed certificate with the mayor's proclamation printed on it and decorated with the seal of the city.

Next the chief of police and the sheriff presented the boys with patches from their departments and another certificate.

Tom was surprised to see Jake walk up to the microphone. "I have the special honor to present a plaque to each of these gentlemen on behalf of the regional office of the FBI." Up until that moment, Tom had no idea that Jake worked for the FBI.

The last person to speak was the publisher of the newspaper. "First I'd like to say that these three boys, who sit before us this afternoon, represent what's good in America today. They are hard workers. Every morning they wake up while much of our city is still sleeping. By the time the sun comes up, they're just finishing their route."

Tom turned to look at his parents. They both smiled back at him.

"I'm going to do something a bit unusual," the publisher continued. "Normally each year we recognize one carrier. That person receives recognition as the best of the best. Well, this morning our executive board met in special session. We've voted not only to move up the date for our recognition, but we've also decided to grant this honor to all three of these fine young men."

The boys looked at each other and grinned.

"And there's one more thing. I happen to know that you boys will be going to the same high school in a couple years. And you plan to go out for football. I also hear it on good authority that you want to attend the same college. So, it is with great pleasure that the newspaper, along with several other agencies in town, are granting you partial scholarships to help with your college expenses."

The crowd applauded and cheered.

"We want you to know we're very proud of each one of you."

Another photographer took several pictures of the boys shaking hands with the mayor and others. Then a huge lunch was served. Tom couldn't remember ever seeing so much food in one place before. When he finally got back home he asked his parents if it would be all right to go visit the lady he'd told them about. He rode his new bike over to her house. As he started down her block he was surprised by what he saw. There, sitting in the woman's driveway was the white Buick. When Tom came closer, he noticed the license plates were back on it too. He stopped his bike next to the car and went to the front door. She must have seen him coming because she opened the door before he could knock or ring the bell.

"Oh, I'm so happy to see you," she sighed. "I just can't believe Agnes is sitting back in my driveway again where she belongs. I'll keep her all locked up tight now." Tears streamed down her wrinkled cheeks. "I'm so grateful to you, Tom."

He just stood there, looking down at his feet.

"The officer who brought my car back said you were the one who found her. Is that true?"

"Sort of."

"And they also gave me a copy of the newspaper. It made me sad to think of all the people who would never see their cars again. If that happened to me, I don't know what I would have done. I know my Harold would be unhappy too."

"I'm just glad it turned out good for you," he told her.

"I haven't taken the paper recently, but I was wondering. Would my house be on your route?"

"Yes it is."

"Could you start the paper for me?" she asked.

"Consider it done." The woman gave Tom a hug and told him again how much she appreciated his kindness. As he rode away from her house, he felt warm inside. It was good to know he had done so much to help so many people. Most of them he would never meet.

It didn't sink in, not all at once, just what had happened. Tom called his friends and the boys gathered at his house later. "We're pretty famous around here," he told them.

"I wonder if any college football scouts read about us, Tom?" Matt asked.

"It's a little early for that, don't you think?"

"Maybe. But everyone in town knows us now."

"That might be true, except tomorrow morning we'll be back on our route like nothing ever happened."

"I don't think things will ever be the same again," Jimmy said.

The next morning, just as Tom had predicted, the newspaper delivery truck dumped stacks of papers in his driveway. His friends rolled in on their new bikes in time to help drag them back to the garage.

Tom began cutting the bundles open. "I can't believe this," he announced. "Two days in a row!"

"Two days in a row for what?" Jimmy asked.

"Our picture. They printed our picture right on the front page again."

"Let me see that," Matt demanded. "This is unbelievable!"

There were several other pictures about the story deeper in the paper. Tom pointed. "Look. That's the man and the woman we saw by the trash can."

Then they looked at their own picture again. "We look pretty good with the mayor and everybody, don't we?" Jimmy crowed.

The boys decided to fold all the papers so their picture stuck right out in front.

"And when we deliver our papers today, everybody

will get to see our picture first," Tom told them.

This morning the boys didn't toss their papers like usual. They took the time to stop at every house and place each paper so their picture was facing straight upand pointing toward the house. That way it's the first thing all their customers would see when they opened their door.

As they rode along one stretch Matt spoke up. "Hey you guys. When we finally get to high school, and we buy that car we're always talking about..."

"You mean the one so we can deliver more papers?" Jimmy asked.

"That's the one. I say we save up some extra money so we can buy every kind of lock and alarm system we can find."

"You're kidding, right?" Tom asked.

"No. I'm totally serious."

"Why bother?"

"So nobody can steal it."

"Trust me," Tom laughed. "The car we buy no one will want to steal. Our car would be the kind a thief would have to bring back and then apologize to us for stealing such a hunk of junk in the first place."

The boys turned down Maple Street. No one thought about it until suddenly that same, mean, pants-eating dog came trotting out from the bushes. He didn't bark. He didn't growl. All he wanted to do was jog along side Matt's bike.

"What is it about us and dogs?" Matt asked.

"I think that one is in love," Jimmy joked.

The dog trotted with them until they rolled past the end of the block. Then he came to a stop, but his tail never quit wagging.

Eventually the boys did go on to high school together. And they did buy a car together so they could deliver more papers, just like they'd planned. After high school they went on to play four years of football at the same college.

None of them made it to the pros.

The entire four years they were away at school, their car stayed parked outside Tom's house. In all that time, no one ever tried to steal the old clunker.

- The End -

MAX ELLIOT ANDERSON

Max Elliot Anderson was a reluctant reader even though he grew up surrounded by books. In fact his father has written more than 70 books. His brothers and sisters liked to read, but that didn't change his lack of interest in books.

Photo by James Brightman

In spite of this he was forced to read and went on to graduate from college with a major in psychology. In 2001 he decided he wanted to discover why he grew up as a reluctant reader. He found an interesting pattern in his search. "In many instances the books I had read defied a person like me to get interested in them. The style was boring, the dialog was sometimes sparse, or when it was used, it seemed too adult. I wanted music, moving pictures, and characters on the screen – not a page of words. I was looking for action, suspense, and humor."

After some time of introspection, he concluded, "Since I still don't like to read, I decided to write a book that I would like." In order to attract and keep readers, he works hard to develop books that will hold interest – especially for reluctant readers or those who think they are.

Anderson has developed an adventure series of books that will hold the interest of tweeners, 8 to13, – especially boys. He describes the series, "It is not a series where all these fantastic things that couldn't possibly happen to any ONE of us, happens to the same kids, in the same town, over and over. My stories all have completely different characters, settings, and adventures."

Mr. Anderson is a Vietnam era veteran of the U.S. Army. His professional life has been spent in the production of films, video programs, and television commercials. He has been involved in the production of some of the most successful Christian films for children including *Hobo and the Runaway*, *The Mystery of Willoubhy Castle*, *The Great Banana Pie Caper*, and many others. His video productions have earned national awards including 3 Telly Awards (the equivalent of the Oscar for movies). He was involved in a PBS television special that won a nomination for an Emmy, and the double album won a Grammy.

He is 56 years old, married with two adult children.

Max Elliot Anderson can be reached at:
P.O. Box 4126, Rockford, IL 61110 email to: Mander8813@aol.com

Other Tweener Books available from Baker Trittin Concepts

Tweener Press Adventure Series

by Max Elliot Anderson

TERROR AT WOLF LAKE - Eddy Thompson was known for one thing and one thing only. Eddy was a cheater. He cheated on anything, anytime, anywhere, until something happened up at Wolf Lake. It wasn't the brutal cold. It wasn't when he fell through the ice. It wasn't even when two scary men arrived at their remote cabin. What happened would change Eddy's like . . . forever.

Other books in the series to be released in 2004:

    NORTH WOODS POACHERS
    MOUNTAIN CABIN MYSTERY
    THE SECRET OF ABBOTT'S CAVE
    BIG-RIG RUSTLERS
    LOST ISLAND SMUGGLERS
    RECKLESS RUNAWAY

Innovative Christian Publications introduces the Gospel Storyteller Series

by Dr. Marvin G. Baker

This series is the "Greatest Story" ever told presented in a conversational story style. It is easily read, clearly understood and enhanced with contemporary illustrations designed to encourage the reader to imagine the "story" taking place in their own neighborhood today. Each book in the five book series serves as an introduction to one of the Gospels or the Book of Acts.

    MARK'S STORY, An Introduction to the
        Gospel of Mark
    MATTHEW'S STORY, An Introduction to the
        Gospel of Matthew

The remaining books will be released in 2004